Hunter's Moon

By

J.E. Taylor

J.E. TAYLOR
SUPERNATURAL SUSPENSE
& DARK FANTASY AUTHOR

Hunter's Moon

A werewolf family saga.

Life handed me a real shitty deal. I'm now bound to a wheelchair for the rest of my life, which sucks for a beta werewolf. Especially one who's in love with my alpha.

She deserves far more than my useless ass.

But she has other ideas. And I can't walk away from her.

Instead of letting me wallow in my misfortune, she puts me in charge of the national werewolf council.

But I can't command respect from a wheelchair.

Will I end up putting a target on our backs again?

CHAPTER 1

I STARED OUT OVER the thick woods from our back deck, wondering how the hell I got here. A light breeze rustled the sparse spring leaves, sending a few of the smaller ones flying in the wind. Anxiety mixed with the heavy pine scent as I pondered my current situation.

Alessandra should have never insisted that I run the werewolf council. I couldn't walk. I couldn't shift without making a fucking fool out of my wolf with my useless hind quarters. How the hell was I supposed to command the respect required to enforce pack laws across the entire continent?

And now she expected me to raise a child.

I was still numb from the news of her pregnancy.

Hell, I hadn't even married her yet. I ran my hand through my hair while I tried to get my bearings. I mean, we'd only slept together a handful of times since fate handed me this shitty paraplegic card.

"Hunter?"

Her voice blanketed me with warmth and terror at the same time. Even if she wasn't my mate, as the alpha of our pack, she couldn't miss my turmoil. The sickly sweet scent of my fear slipped out of my pores.

When her hands landed on my shoulders, I stiffened under her soft touch. I refused to look up at her.

"You will make a fantastic father."

I scoffed at her and glanced up at her. She had her long, dark hair in a braid as she did any time she cooked. Her blue-eyed gaze pierced right to the depths of my soul.

"You are out of your mind." I couldn't keep the words from tumbling from my mouth. "I can't shift. I can't teach my kid to hunt." I bit down the rest of the words at the flare of hurt through our bond and its presence in the watery glaze forming over her eyes.

"Being a father takes more than just running in the woods." She turned and headed back inside in a huff.

I maneuvered my wheelchair and followed her inside. "I get that. But I can't even do the simplest things. I can't protect a child." I waved my hand at her. "I can't even protect you."

Her eyes narrowed at me. "You know how to shoot." She nodded to the hardware attached to my chair.

What the hell was she thinking? "Yeah, and having a gun within reach of a child is reasonable." I couldn't help the sarcasm dripping from every word.

"Well, I'm not getting rid of it." She crossed her arms, and her tight-lipped expression filled with her fiery, stubborn resolve.

That was the look I couldn't fight. The one that shut me down. I had no chance in hell of swaying my alpha, and as her beta, I had to come to heel. The growl forming in her throat challenged me to say otherwise.

I lowered my gaze and nodded once. There was so much more I wanted to say, but it would just push her buttons, and I couldn't defend against her hormonal wolf.

"I guess we should get married," I mumbled under my breath.

"Don't sound so excited about it."

I snapped my gaze up to hers as my hackles rose in aggravation. I could feel my teeth elongating and I clenched my mouth closed before I shifted into my wolf out of sheer exasperation. "This is not what I envisioned."

"You've had enough time to design the perfect proposal."

"I've had six weeks. That isn't enough time." I knew it was just an excuse. I didn't believe an alpha should be subjected to a life with a cripple. Especially one as hot and smart as Alessandra.

"Do you even love me?" she shouted.

"I've killed for you. I've run from the law for you. I've nearly died for you. I fucking love you more than anything, and that's why I haven't asked."

Her eyes widened.

"You don't need to be saddled with someone like me for the rest of your days." I rolled past her toward my office, but she swung me back so I was facing her.

Her eyes shined with tears and raged with anger at the same time. "Jacob Randall Blaez, I don't care that you are in a wheelchair. It doesn't change who you are."

Oh, she pulled out the big guns by using my given name, not the nickname everyone else called me for as long as I could remember. "That's easy for you to say. You can still let your wolf out to run. I can't. I'm damaged!" I yelled in her face, fisting my hands and slamming them on the twigs of my legs. "I'm useless."

She grabbed a fistful of my hair and yanked my head back. "Don't you ever say that."

Her command wrapped around me. "You deserve more," I snarled through my clenched teeth.

She closed her eyes and tilted her head back, taking a deep breath, before she returned her gaze to mine. "Jake," she started, and the use of the nickname she used while we were on the run stole my ability to breathe. "You are the only one there is for me. And I don't care about your disability. It's you I love." She poked my chest with her free hand before covering whatever words I was going to hurl at her with her mouth.

Her tongue tangled with mine as she slid onto my lap, and I forgot every point of argument. Even though I've loved her forever, I still didn't think she should settle for me. But I was her beta, and I would serve her until the day I died.

CHAPTER 2

ALESSANDRA'S DISTRACTION DIDN'T DISSUADE me from my original thoughts. She didn't understand how unprepared to be a father I was. Hell, I took two to three hours to even be presentable in the mornings. My new humiliating reality included a fucking bowel program, so I didn't shit my pants later in the day.

I learned *that* lesson pretty quick.

Being confined to a wheelchair for the last six months had been more of a wake-up call as to what the rest of my life would be like. I wasn't sure I could saddle my alpha with this burden. There were plenty of eligible wolves in our pack, and the council had access to many more.

My routine was grueling enough without throwing a wife and child into the mix. And although Alessandra wanted to help, I could not allow it. I didn't need her to be my nursemaid.

I rolled my wheelchair into my office while she went back to preparing our dinner. I carefully inserted myself behind the desk, making sure I was in the center where the drawer was at its thinnest. I'd misaligned before and found massive bruises from the desk pressing on my legs when I undressed that night. It wasn't fun trying to explain to Alessandra that I hadn't felt the desk doing the damage she saw.

That was my existence. Bruises and cuts on my legs could kill me. And if I wasn't careful, I would develop sores on my ass from not moving for hours on end. It was obnoxious. It was a damn hazard.

And God forbid if we were ever attacked again. I'd be a liability, despite what Alessandra or the other pack members said. And that weighed heavily on me.

Which meant I had to be extra vigilant. Not only here at home, but on the council. The judgments we rendered had to fit the crimes laid before us. Anything else but just sentencing and we'd be targeted.

Sometimes, I had to make tough calls that put me on some wolf's shit list. It wasn't easy, especially with my vulnerabilities exposed for all to see.

Then there was the Monster Defense Agency. Run by Winters's brother, of all people. If Terrance Winters didn't run that agency, I would have gladly opted for a more global organization to oversee the laws of pack life. But I didn't trust him, despite his denouncements of his brother's atrocities.

If I wasn't careful with how I operated the council, the Monster Defense Agency might decide that we were within its domain, like they had done to some packs in the area around the city.

The pressure of being the leader of the werewolf council, coupled with my condition, exhausted me. And now I had to find the energy to raise a child?

I mopped my face with my hand, grumbling to myself. I leaned back and ran my fingers through my hair before I looked out into the belly of our house. If I hadn't been confined to a wheelchair for the rest of my life, the news she gave me would have made my heart soar.

I closed my eyes and opened my mind to our connection. I hadn't done it since the accident because I didn't want to know what Alessandra was feeling. I didn't want her pity at my sorry state. I clenched my teeth at the hurt that radiated from her; just below that was anger. And below that was the love she felt that kept her tied to me.

I sighed and moved away from the desk. I had been the one to pull away, and she let me because she thought I needed space to come to grips with this news. But my reaction made her miserable.

Fuck.

I reached into the drawer and took out the little box that I had bought weeks ago when I thought maybe I'd get the feeling back in my legs, and from there be able to walk again. But the tingling in my toes hadn't occurred since. The doctors said it was a ghost tingle, which happens with paraplegics and amputees.

After that news, I couldn't bring myself to give it to her.

I went in search of her and found her chopping carrots in the kitchen. Well, it looked more like massacring the carrot bits, but I would not comment while she held a fast-moving blade. I waited until she finished this round of kill the carrot and cleared my throat the minute she put the sharp kitchen utensil down.

"I'm sorry." I met her gaze and shrugged. "If it weren't for this" —I patted the arms of my wheelchair—"I would be ecstatic." I licked my lips under her sharp stare. "And I would have already married you."

Her eyes narrowed, and she grabbed the carrots, tossing them into a pan. "So, I get a raw deal because you did?" Her words came out in a snarl.

"Being saddled with me *is* a raw deal."

The muscles in her jaw jumped. "Am I not enough for you?"

I blinked and pressed back in my chair. Her words cut as effectively as the kitchen knife she had been using on the carrot. "It's not you who isn't enough, Leigh, and you damn well know that."

Tears bloomed in her eyes, and one rolled down her cheek.

Double fuck.

"What happens now?" Another tear slid down her cheek.

Defeat scraped my skin. I hated when Alessandra cried. It broke me more than this fucking chair I was chained to. And I loved her. I just didn't want her to be stuck with me for the rest of her life. I rolled to the counter and put the box on the edge across from her, and then moved back to where the kitchen turned into the living area.

"I can't sweep you off your feet." I looked at the ground, trying to find the right words. "But if this is what you want to settle for..." I glanced back at her with a wince. "I'll give you the best that I can." The entire proposal sucked. There were no rose petals leading to me with the ring box. No soft music. No candlelight. Nothing but my lame offer and a ring.

Just like the course of my life, my plans changed drastically the moment that car overturned down the embankment and the crash shattered my spine.

She looked at the box as if it might bite her, but after a moment reached over and snatched it as if I might change my mind. When she snapped the box open, her eyes widened and her gaze jumped to mine.

"I got it after..." I waved at her, and my cheeks heated. "I thought the tingling meant I might regain feeling in my legs." I let out a bitter laugh. "Then I got the news that it was a fluke. Ghost tingles, like an amputee."

She closed the box and put it on the counter before she leveled a glare at me.

My heart dropped.

CHAPTER 3

THE WAY HER LIPS pursed, as she considered my failed proposal, left me fidgeting in my wheelchair.

"Is this what you want?"

If she had asked me before I put the ring on the counter, I might have said something sarcastic, but with her intense stare settled on me, I chewed on my lower lip. I had already made my feelings known about what I wanted for her. But I probably would waste away to nothing if she left. I loved her enough to let her go if she didn't want this life, but I also couldn't see my life without her.

"For purely selfish reasons, yes," I whispered.

She rolled her eyes and turned back to the roast, putting it back in the oven before she wiped her hands and faced me again.

"Then ask me the proper way." She crossed her arms, waiting.

I ran my hand through my hair and sighed before I rolled the chair around the island and faced her. I couldn't reach the box where she had placed it, so I put my hand out for it, staring her down.

She slammed it in my palm and crossed her arms again, silently daring me to follow through, as if she didn't believe I actually would.

I took a slow and the inhale and blew it out in a long stream, getting the right words in place in my head before I looked up at her.

"Leah," I started with the nickname I had used for her when we were on the run. "I love you. And while I don't want to saddle you with my situation, I cannot see my life without you by my side to kick my ass into next week when I'm wallowing in self-pity."

Her lip twitched up on one side.

"As I said before, I can't sweep you off your feet or slow dance with you in my arms, but I can try to give you my best in other ways." My lips curved at the thoughts of how much she liked my mouth and my hands on her. I had gotten very good at hitting all the right spots to make her squirm and cry out my name.

Blush shaded her cheeks.

"I'd give anything to shift and run with you again, but you'll just have to settle for my endless adoration instead." I opened the box. "Will you spend the next however long we have at my side as my wife?"

This time, her hand fluttered to her lips and her eyes teared up again. And to my eternal relief, she nodded.

"Yes, Jake. I'll marry you." Her husky voice bled from behind her splayed fingers.

I took the diamond solitaire out of the box, and she stuck her left hand out. I slid it on her ring finger and leaned back in the chair. It wasn't what I had envisioned, but the teary smirk she gave me made up for my lack of finesse.

"Now, was that so hard?" She held out her hand and scrutinized the ring before smiling at me.

I gave her my *cut the crap* look and rolled backward. My emotional reaction wasn't what I expected, either. Right alongside the relief was a healthy dose of fear, as if I had sentenced her to a life of pain and anguish.

She sniffled and then blinked at me. Her head cocked to the right side and that line between her eyes creased deeper. "What are you afraid of?"

I laughed, trying to shake the certainty of pending doom. "Regrets."

Her eyebrows rose, and she shook her head. "My only regret was that I didn't realize how you felt about me sooner." She glanced down at the ring. "If I had, you'd still be able to walk."

"Or I'd be dead by Winters's hand." I wouldn't have been able to let that whole situation go. Not with the information my father left me, and she knew it.

Her face paled enough for me to sigh and move toward her. I knew where her mind drifted. I had seen those awful silver statues, too. She didn't know, but I made Nathan take me down there before those hideous things were removed. I needed to see what had been done to my parents and to let them know I'd avenged their deaths.

I wrapped my arms around her waist and pulled her down onto my lap. "My regrets have nothing to do with the past and more to do with the future. I wanted more for you than my sorry ass." Before she could argue, I pulled her lips to mine, silencing her with a kiss.

She melted into me, and the kiss lingered, warming my blood and teasing my nerves. But it only lasted for a few moments before she pulled away.

"There is no one else out there for me. Or for you." She met my gaze and poked my chest to bring home her point. And although I had fooled around before her, it never felt right. As frustratingly blind as she had been for years, the only time I felt complete was when I was near this beautiful woman.

I had never told her that, and I wasn't sure I could leave myself that vulnerable by spilling that piece of my heart. Not when she had all the rest of it laid bare. I loved the woman, but I needed that last shred of dignity to remain intact.

CHAPTER 4

NO ONE EVER TOLD me how amazing childbirth was. I sat by Alessandra's side, alternating between holding her hand and then holding her leg behind the knee when she had to push. I stared at the crop of black hair as it crested her opening, and my heart nearly seized in my chest.

Alessandra panted and pushed until the baby's shoulders breeched, and then the doctor pulled the baby out of her womb.

"You have a boy!" the doctor announced.

I swear, my heart grew in my chest with the amount of love that filled me in that moment. I was in utter awe of my wife and the baby. Enough so when the doctor handed me the surgical scissors, I stared at him, dumbfounded.

"Would you like to cut the cord, Mr. Blaez?"

I blinked and glanced at the loop of umbilical cord he held. I took the scissors and cut where the doctor instructed me to, and then the baby was taken to be cleaned and weighed and measured.

"Do you have a name?" the delivery room nurse asked.

"Archer. Archer Henry Blaez," Alessandra said.

My heart expanded with pride. We had discussed which of our father's names would be first, and she initially wanted her father's first. But she must have changed her mind at the last minute.

I looked over at my father's namesake as he wailed on the table. I wanted to go to him, but Alessandra gripped my hand as another contraction had her gasping.

"Is this normal?" I asked the doctor.

He nodded. "The placenta." He pulled out a rubbery bloody thing that had housed my son for the last nine months. The doctor put it in an empty clear pan on the table to the side of us.

Before I gave in and poked the placenta to see whether it indeed felt as rubbery as it looked, the nurse brought Archer to Alessandra and laid him in my wife's arms. I stared at them and smiled, forgetting all my misgivings about being a father. It didn't matter because I would go feral for that child if I had to.

Alessandra looked up from our son's little face and grinned. She had never looked so exhausted or radiant. "Archer," she said to the baby in her arms and pressed a kiss to his forehead.

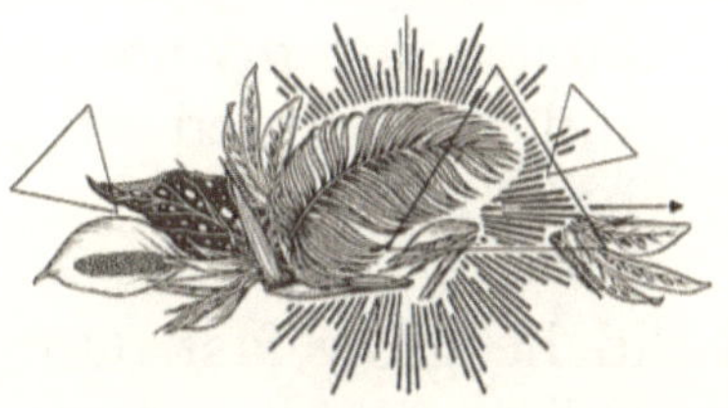

THE NOVELTY OF A child wore off quick once we arrived home with our little bundle of joy, and my limitations soon became glaringly apparent. Don't get me wrong. I loved the little guy. But I couldn't get him out of the damn crib from a wheelchair. The changing table was too tall and even trying to change him on the couch or the bed once he started rolling was more of a challenge than I thought it would be.

Plus, getting on the floor to play with him wasn't an option without a handful of the pack members here to pick me up and put me back in the chair. If my legs were amputated, I might be able to get myself up with no issues. But my legs were dead weight I couldn't maneuver easily.

God knows I've done it before, like the time a nightmare caused me to fling myself out of the bed. Alessandra had been out late at a pack meeting, so I had no one to help me get back to the bed. It took a bit to get into my wheelchair and then into the bed. Much longer than a parent has when dealing with a mobile infant or toddler.

But even with the less-than-ideal situation, I found there were moments with my son that I would not trade for anything in all the world. Like when he fell asleep on my shoulder or when I read to him and he pointed at the pictures when I named what they were.

And damn did he grow fast. One minute he was in diapers and the next he was eleven and coming into his wolf. Unfortunately, he didn't have the mark of the alpha like his mother, but that didn't keep him from dreaming.

ARCHER RAN AROUND THE backyard with the girl from down the street before the school bus came to pick them up. Alessandra stepped next to me at the sliding doors and handed me a cold beer. She sighed, and I glanced up at her. Melancholy etched into her features.

"We used to run around like that." She nodded at the kids outside.

"Yeah, well, you married my sorry ass." I turned my attention to my son and his girlfriend.

"I know. But I was talking about Archer and me. Not us." She whacked my arm lightly with the back of her hand.

I just grunted, acknowledging her statement. But I would have given my left nut to do that now.

"I miss running in the woods with you. It was the highlight of my youth."

I raised my eyebrow at her. "You could have fooled me. You tried to get out of every pack run possible," I teased. After all, once she went off to college, she nearly cut us all off just to find herself. And look what that cost us.

She smirked. "Yeah, well…" Color crept into her cheeks. "I was kind of a brat back then, wasn't I?"

"Don't make me answer that." I smiled up at her and poked her in the side. Archer's friend was cute with dark hair like Archer, but her eyes were a different color blue. Archer had Alessandra's eyes but seemed like he was going to have my build. Well, my former build. Anyway, Alessandra said he looked like I did when I was his age.

She was studying the two wolves in the backyard, playing as if there wasn't a care in the world. "I hope he ends up with an alpha by his side."

I agreed. Even with Alessandra training him to be a leader, she couldn't give him the alpha position. In other packs, the alpha position was passed down within the family unless a challenge was made. Then there would be a fight to the death for the position. Being the child of an alpha didn't make it a given in our pack. Only the member with the leader symbol was viewed as the alpha. And it only appeared on those who were worthy of the position.

Alessandra had been magically branded with the stamp of a leader the day she saved me from a vat of silver.

Her father had the same mystical tattoo on his forearm, but his had appeared early on. Hers only appeared after defeating the council. And the next alpha in our pack would be branded the same way. She had deferred leading the council to me because she felt she had zero political savvy.

And somehow, I kept us out of the oversight of the Monster Defense Agency. Although they visited once a year to compare notes. Until recently, I had dealt with Terrance Winters. Every time I got near that man; I had to lock down my wolf. Terrance's brother's actions had put me in this wheelchair, and as much as I wanted to peg Terrance as the same, he didn't seem to be.

He couldn't shift, so he wasn't as critical of a threat as his brother had been. Even so, I was sure he was keeping secrets of his own. Secrets that would turn the council against him if they ever came to light.

The last couple of years, he came with a sullen wolf who had haunted eyes that reminded me of my own. This past year, Terrance told us that Robert Young of the Allegany pack would represent him in these annual reviews of pack laws.

And Robert Young called to ask for a private meeting with me, without the council and without my pack's alpha. Easier said than done considering I was married to the alpha, but his request scratched at my curiosity enough that I agreed.

Thankfully, I still had my driver's license and a car made specifically for paraplegics. I wasn't housebound, but I'd have to figure out a reason to go off on my own, which was rare.

I glanced at my watch and then at the kids outside. "I need to run out for a few." I rolled away from the back slider.

Alessandra raised her eyebrow. "Where are you going?"

"I will be back before dinner." I just smiled and left it at that.

Thankfully, the Allegany pack alpha had requested a meeting near Alessandra's birthday, and where I suggested the meeting was in the middle of a shopping mall far enough away from most of the pack that the likelihood of being seen was low. So, I could pick out a gift she wouldn't find delivered on the doorstep.

The cryptic way he had sounded on the phone didn't fill me with warm and fuzzies, but he insisted I meet him. I just hoped going alone wasn't a mistake.

CHAPTER 5

I ARRIVED AT THE coffee shop early to account for the time it would take me to get out of the car and into the quaint shop. If I didn't know better, I would have thought the place was packed based on the long line of cars at the takeout window. But thankfully, there was only one table occupied inside.

I ordered a coffee at the counter and rolled to a table in the far corner, away from the counter and at the farthest point from the other person, and took the space that faced the door.

The barista was kind enough to deliver my coffee to me instead of just calling my name. The moment she stepped away, Robert Young stepped inside with another person trailing a step behind him. He handed the woman a bill and nodded toward the counter.

I sniffed, trying to detect whether she was a wolf, but all I smelled was Robert's unique hemlock scent and her human sweat aroma. I met Robert's gaze as he approached. His usually neat hair looked as if he had repeatedly raked his hand through it on the drive here. And he seemed more nervous than a groom at a shotgun wedding.

Robert Young fell into the chair across from me. "I hope like hell I've pegged you right."

A low growl came from my throat as I raised my eyebrows. "I came alone like you asked and lied to my wife in the process."

Robert ran his hand through his hair. "At least your wife is safe. Mine was killed by the agency, along with my kids."

I sat back in my chair, rolling it with the action. "Excuse me?"

"Terrance Winters is just as fucked up as his brother." His voice rumbled from his chest. "And he is in league with the vampires."

"Why haven't you brought this up with the council?" My mind couldn't wrap around the venom coming from this man. Especially with how docile and under control he seemed over the years when he accompanied Terrance to the council meetings.

He laughed. "If I had, the council would have been slaughtered." He leaned forward. "It has taken me years to earn Terrance's trust. And because I pretended to be his lackey for so long, I am in the position to figure out a plan to bring the bastard down, along with the damn agency." He looked at the coffee line where the woman he was with stood, spouting off their order. "And save some lives in the process." He turned back to me. "That's where you come in."

I pointed at my chest in surprise, still digesting his little speech.

"I need people to disappear."

My mind closed down. I crossed my arms. "I don't kill people."

His smile was sarcastic, and he leaned forward into my personal space, speaking so softly that only a wolf could hear. "No, I need them to disappear into the world. I need new identities and places where they will be safe from the retribution of the agency."

I blinked and glanced around and then back at him as everything he said processed slowly. "What exactly am I protecting them from?"

"Unjustified murder."

I pursed my lips. Being on the council taught me that justification varied from person to person. What one may feel was unjust mighty actually be valid. "Define what you feel is unjustified."

"Being sentenced to die because of a relationship with another agent. Or wanting to leave the agency. Or letting a target go because the facts don't support killing them like we are ordered." He cocked his head. "Or using boiling silver to threaten and control wolves, or to torture and kill them if they are not complying with agency rules."

Heat fled my face. Torturing werewolves with boiling silver had been outlawed in the United States. That was the first law I put into effect, and Terrance Winters knew that.

"Shall I go on?"

"No. You've made your point." My gaze moved to the woman approaching with coffee. Her pale eyes held hope and her hands shook as she gave Robert his coffee. "But how do you know this is happening?" I couldn't just take his word. I needed more than that.

"I was promoted to the position of agency enforcer. I'm supposed to kill these people and bring proof back to Winters." Bitterness framed every word.

My insides turned. "You've killed our kind?"

"I've been able to avoid it so far. But I've been forced to witness enough gruesome deaths to want to help others." He glanced at woman still standing next to him. He waved her to the adjoining chair. "This is Stacy. She didn't follow through on an order to kill and her partner ratted her out. I'm supposed to kill her, but I want you to secure a new identity for her and help her get a new life."

I looked her over and then moved my gaze to Robert as everything hit with the force of a flying brick. Thankfully, none of our wolves ever signed on to work in the Monster Defense business.

"Witch?" I asked. It was well known that witches and wolves were paired together in the agency.

Stacy nodded as her eyes darted around the room, looking for a sign of anything wrong.

"Will you help me?" Robert asked.

I stared at him and then looked around the café. The man who had been in the far corner had left soon after Robert arrived, and it was only us and the staff serving the takeout window. Agreeing to this without really thinking it over made me uncomfortable. Although saving innocent lives was a righteous endeavor, this could paint another target on me and my family.

"I have a wife and a young son. Will this put them in danger?"

Robert closed his eyes and hung his head. "If the agency finds out what I'm doing, yes." He took a breath and opened his eyes. "If they find out, my son will die. I've come to heel to the agency to save that boy. He's all I have left. You are not the only one risking everything."

My gaze narrowed. "I thought you said the agency killed your kids."

He nodded. "My oldest and middle child were slaughtered. By dumb luck, my youngest was at a sleepover for his friend's birthday. If he had been home, he would have died, too."

"And you didn't kill Winters?" I couldn't fathom letting the man walk if he harmed my family.

"He threatened to kill my son if I didn't straighten up. So no, I didn't kill him. Besides, while he's as screwed up as Ken was, he's not the top dog running the show. The agency has vampires and other ancient beings pulling the strings." He wiped a hand down his face.

"Vampires?" Mangy beasts that drained others of blood. We were their food as much as humans were. "I thought the agency put vampires down?"

Robert laughed. "Only those that the vampires sanction. It's not black and white like the agency makes it sound. They are snowing you, appeasing you and the council, so they have a chance at recruiting more wolves. My pack isn't under the rule of your council. And there are others that aren't either. They are bound to sacrificing their members to the damned agency."

"But they honor the annual gatherings. You've been here with him and gone over the rules that werewolves are supposed to live by." I blinked, thinking about how many years we had gone through the rule book with the head of the agency in attendance. And how that bastard always had spoken down to me, as if he thought he was better than all of us. Righteous anger filled me, and I stared at Robert.

"Yeah. I was part of that ruse." He had the sense to look remorseful. "But now that I'm not under his watch all the time, I have the latitude to keep you informed of what is really going on. And if something happens to me, I'd want you to talk with my son. I don't want him to be trapped in the agency once he comes of age."

"And what of your pack?"

His jaw tightened, and he shook his head. "The new alpha would have to make that determination. But the agency has several hooks into the pack already, so I don't know that they'd be able to break free."

"Your son wouldn't be named alpha?"

Robert hung his head. "He has the ability to be a phenomenal alpha. He's a natural leader, even as a teenager, but it would put him in the direct line of fire of the agency. I might not have a say in his future, but I'd like some assurances that if I die, someone with values and honor outside of my pack will step in and take care of my boy."

That was an enormous sacrifice. One which made me understand the true magnitude of what was going on. Everything up to this point had warning bells clanging in my head, but asking another pack to take in your child if something happened made me take all this seriously. That just wasn't done.

"Just so I am clear. If something happens to you, you want Alessandra and me to raise him?" He'd likely never be an alpha in our pack unless the magic surrounding the mark made that decision.

Robert did not hesitate. "Yes."

I slowly nodded. Alessandra would take him into our pack if disaster struck, and we still had control of the council, so we had the power of most of the packs in the nation behind us to make that happen.

"So, about Stacy?" Robert asked.

I licked my lips and sighed. I couldn't in good conscience let her die now that I'd looked into her eyes and smelled her fear. "Where do you want to go?"

She blinked at me, and her mouth popped open. "You are going to help?"

My lips tilted into a smile. Hope flared in her features, brightening her eyes. "Yes. Robert makes a very compelling argument. So, where do you want to go?"

"Go?"

"You can't stay with my pack. That's too dangerous. But I can help you with a new identity and at least get you to a destination of your choosing. Then it is up to you." I had some questionable people that my father had connected me with before he disappeared, and I had kept contact with them over the years. I had an exit plan in place if our lives ever went to shit again. They had the ability to create identities for me at the drop of a hat. And they were discreet enough that word would not get out.

"Anywhere but New York," Stacy said.

I swiveled my gaze to Robert. "This will not be a weekly thing, right?"

He shook his head. "No. I might not get the chance to do this again, but Stacy has been a friend of mine since the academy. I think Terrance did this to test me again. Anyway." He turned to Stacy. "I'll need your wallet and your agency ID." He put his hand out.

Stacy handed both items over. "What are you going to do?"

Robert stared at her and then turned to me. "Thanks," he said before he stood and left the shop.

I glanced at Stacy. "Why did you ask that?"

"Because there has to be a body."

"Meaning?"

"He's going to have to kill someone and make the authorities think the body is mine." She stared at the door and shivered. "But at least he'll find someone who deserves it. He doesn't kill innocents. Ever."

I had killed before, so I knew the price that exacted on a soul. I just hoped he'd make it happen as far from our pack lands as possible. "I need to pick out a gift for my wife for her birthday." I rolled back from the table. "And then I have to figure out what to do with you."

She remained seated until I stopped and spun toward her. "Are you coming?"

"Oh. You want me to come along with you?"

"Yeah. I'm not just going to leave you in a coffee shop." I gave her my best "duh" expression and then rolled out onto the sidewalk with her at my side. "What kind of magic do you have?" I asked as we rolled toward a jewelry store.

"I have scouring magic."

I glanced at her. "That really means nothing to me."

"The easiest way to explain it is I can scour a room of grime just as easily as I can wipe a mind clean."

I slowed to a stop as a fantastic idea came to mind. One that would give me time to get her a new identity and give Alessandra a gift that I know she'd appreciate, even if it was only for a couple of months.

Stacy side-eyed me. "What?" she asked, as if she saw the wheels in motion in my head.

"Look, I was going to get my wife some jewelry for her birthday, but I still would have to explain you. So, how do you feel about cleaning our house for the next month while I work on getting you that new identity?"

"I thought you didn't want me staying with your pack."

I sighed. "I don't, but I can't exactly leave you somewhere on your own where you could draw attention and get yourself killed. My home is secluded enough to be off the agency's radar. Besides, I have a finished apartment over our garage for visiting alphas and their families. No one is scheduled to be there for a while."

"Rob said you had a run-in with Winters's brother?" She shifted her stance, studying me.

I snorted a laugh and nodded. "You could say that. Ken Winters killed my parents and put me in this damn wheelchair." I started rolling toward the stores again. "Do I need to pick out a necklace for my wife, or would you be our new house cleaner for a short time?"

"They can track my magic."

I sighed and rubbed my face. "Okay, then how about doing it for real instead of with your magic?"

Her eyebrows rose.

"I know. You're a big, bad Monster Defense agent. But it buys me time to get what I need to get you a new identity and gives my wife a break. As you can see, I'm not very helpful around the house." I waved at the chair. "I try, but I just irritate the shit out of her."

For the first time since she walked into the coffee shop, Stacy smiled. Her freckled cheeks pitted with dimples, and she swept her honey-blonde hair over her shoulder. "Fine. But you might want to get your wife that necklace. My manual cleaning skills are rusty as hell."

CHAPTER 6

WE ROLLED INTO THE driveway as the school bus pulled away. Archer stood at the front door and even from here, I could see the cock of his eyebrow as Stacy stepped out of the passenger seat.

She waited for me to get in my chair and roll to the front door.

Alessandra stood at the door with her arms crossed and her gaze drifting between us.

"Happy birthday a little early," I said as I made up a new identity for Stacy on the fly.

"Rosie Beeswich, this is my wife Alessandra and my son Archer." I waved between the group as I tucked the jewelry bag into the side of the chair. I turned to my wife. "Rosie is our new maid. She'll stay in the apartment above the garage for the time that I hired her for."

Alessandra stared at me. I shifted in the seat and kept her gaze, hoping she would buy this.

"It's nice to meet you, Mrs. Blaez." Stacy stuck her hand out without missing a beat. "Mr. Blaez said you'd be able to show me to the apartment?"

I was impressed. She must have seen the stairway in the garage. Stairs I couldn't climb in a wheelchair.

"Sure, just as soon as we finish dinner. I made enough for an army, so you're welcome to join us." Alessandra waved her inside and then gave me a *what the fuck* look.

I held out the car keys to Archer. "Her suitcase is in the backseat of the car. Can you bring it up to the garage apartment?"

Archer grumbled but went and did what I asked.

"So, where did my husband find you?"

"Through Holly Maid. It's a national maid service that matches maids with households in need." She smiled. "I was looking for a live-in opportunity since rent has gone insane the last few years. And this will give me a chance to get back on my feet."

I wanted to ask how she knew that, but I guess her using my phone for web searches on the ride back had a point. She must have been studying up on a cover story for the ride home.

My wife glanced at me. "Get back on your feet?"

Stacy licked her lips and glanced at me before she looked at Alessandra. "I recently got out of an abusive relationship." She looked at the ground and then back up. "I've been living in shelters and working locally, but I needed a change of scenery, and this job offered the perfect opportunity to start over."

Based on what Robert had said about the agency, this really wasn't that much of a lie.

"Well, I'm glad my husband found you. We could use the extra hand around here." She glanced around the house. The only thing out of place were the magazines on the coffee table. Everything else here was neat enough, but that's only because she took pristine care of the place.

She led us into the kitchen and put another place setting on the table.

I excused myself and rolled into the bedroom to hide the necklace I had gotten. If Stacy was that lame in cleaning, I'd need to have something to appease Alessandra. I still didn't know whether to clue her into the truth, but I certainly wouldn't broach that subject until we were alone and Archer was fast asleep.

I wasn't sure whether Alessandra would slap me or hug me for taking this on. But I knew damned well she'd want to take out Winters. That condescending bastard was breaking the rules and being such a barbaric dick.

I'd have to tell her, eventually. But until then, she'd have a little less work to do around the house. I just hoped all this wouldn't backfire.

CHAPTER 7

IT WAS WELL PAST midnight, and the possible consequences of helping Stacy kept me awake. I studied the ceiling as if it would give me magical answers, but it was just paint and spackle and imparted zero knowledge.

"What's bothering you?" Alessandra asked, pulling my attention to her.

I wiped my face and then glanced at her, weighing my options. I decided to come clean because my brain couldn't work fast enough at this hour to provide a convincing lie. "Robert Young asked for a private meeting today."

Her sleepy eyes widened, and she propped up on her elbow. She had never been comfortable with the idea of the Monster Defense Agency. And although she knew it was required of them to attend the annual standing meeting with the council, she never really felt comfortable in Terrance's presence. But she had been curious about the alpha he dragged around with him over the years.

"Why didn't he come to me?" she asked as that crease of irritation formed between her eyes.

Protocol for visiting alphas made it clear they should meet with the head of the pack before coming into pack territory. Otherwise, it could be seen as encroachment.

Her irritation raked over my skin. I glanced at her and sighed. "I know Robert didn't follow protocol. But he wasn't here to challenge your territory."

"Then why did he ask for a meeting?" The clip in her voice and the way her eyes went to a darker shade of blue announced her aggravation.

"It seems Terrance didn't fall far from his brother, after all."

She blanched and her exposed skin broke out into goose flesh. Her gaze narrowed, and her lips thinned. Anger radiated from her, brushing my skin with its heat. "What's he doing?"

I didn't want to explain the particulars and send her into a frenzy. "So many unscrupulous things. Enough for Robert to ask for our help smuggling people out of the agency."

Her eyebrows rose. "Why don't they just quit?"

I pinched the bridge of my nose, wondering whether he was actually playing me. They knew torture and death by liquid silver were outlawed. That was the first pack law I put in place when I took over as the council head. And Robert was versed in our history with Ken Winters enough to play that card, knowing I would react the way I did.

"According to Robert, once you're in, that's it. There's no getting out."

In the wee hours of the night, my acceptance of the situation seemed just as ludicrous as his story. I glanced at Alessandra. She blinked, and I knew all the pieces were falling into place.

"Rosie?"

"Her name is Stacy, but we're going to get her a full identity matching the name I came up with on the fly." I chewed my bottom lip, waiting for Alessandra to lose her cool with me.

"Why isn't Robert doing something about it?"

The snap in her voice tugged at my core.

"He can't. It seems the agency has some powerful benefactors calling the shots and when he stepped out of line and disobeyed the rules, they killed his wife and two of his three kids."

She sucked in a breath and her fingers fluttered over her mouth as her wide eyes stared at me.

That in itself was a reason to go after the bastards, but we did not have the power to take on an army of supernaturals. Not even if we had all the packs in the werewolf council backing us.

"And if he doesn't play the faithful employee, they'll go after his remaining son," I added as my first comment settled in.

She covered her eyes with her arm and flopped back on the pillow. Anger and sorrow leaked through our bond.

I'm sure her mind went where mine did on hearing all this. I would do anything to keep my son safe. "He asked if we'd take his son in if anything happens to him."

Her gaze whipped to mine. "Wouldn't his son be the alpha of their pack?"

I nodded. "But that would damn him to be under the control of the agency." He sighed. "And if they find out we are involved in helping the agents get new identities, we'll likely be targets again." I met her gaze.

She studied the ceiling the same way I had been doing for most of the night.

I expected an argument. We had lost so much to Ken Winters and his quest for power. Both our parents, and my ability to walk, were stolen from us by that bastard.

"Is there anything else we can do?" she asked softly, surprising the hell out of me.

"Not without putting our family in danger."

She scoffed at me, and her fierce glare moved to me. Her unsettled itch to exact justice filled every pore. If I didn't lay this out in a way that she could grasp, she was likely to go after Winters without backup. And although she had won the last war we had with that family, it had cost us a lot more than just a few scratches.

"He doesn't want us in the crosshairs of the agency. He asked that we just shield and save those he funnels to us. If we get involved beyond being *'the wizard behind the curtain,'* we'll be screwed, and Robert will lose his son and likely his own life." I framed the wizard saying in finger quotes. "The agency's allies include vampires. They aren't things I want to tango with. Especially not in my condition." I waved at my useless lower half. "Robert wants to keep our involvement at a minimum, so he has a haven for his son. But he can't save these people alone."

She moved her gaze to the ceiling again as she digested the situation. Her turmoil bled through our bond, but the scrunch of her forehead and then the long sigh announced her acceptance of the situation more than the soft "Okay" she whispered before she rolled toward me and fluffed her pillow up under her cheek.

It was my turn to blink at her. I expected more of a fight, especially considering I put us in the middle of this mess. "You're not mad?"

She palmed my cheek. "Your heart's in the right place."

I waited for more. When it didn't come, I said, "But...?"

"No buts. I would have done the same. But where are you going to find the right contacts to get fake IDs?" She searched my gaze.

I grinned. I had quite a few reliable—if questionable—alliances that I could tap into to help. She just didn't know about them. My father had connected me to a lot of different sources in the event I had to go on the run. I just hadn't had the chance to reach out when we were on the run, but I had kept in contact over the years.

"I do." I didn't expand further. She didn't need to know how fully prepared I was for another catastrophic event. I would not leave us in the dark and on the run without a plan again.

"We also need to build stronger alliances with all the packs who are not involved in the agency, so we are all protected from their insidiousness. Once they get their foot in the door, they own the pack. And I don't want them anywhere near any of ours."

CHAPTER 8

STACY STAYED WITH US for a couple of months while I sorted out her documentation. She wasn't the best maid in the world, but she helped Alessandra a lot, lifting her home burdens much more than I could. She also helped Archer with some of his more difficult math and science homework while I worked my ass off on setting up a solid network to tap into whenever I needed.

Archer was the only person in the house who did not truly know where she came from. And we had agreed to keep it that way.

Alessandra kept the secret from the pack as well. This was not something that should be broadcast widely. It needed to be conducted in secrecy, so our wards survived. If anyone slipped, it would put the pack at the Monster Defense Agency's mercy. And she reached out to the other alphas, building more powerful alliances, just like I asked her to do. She also influenced several of them to avoid giving in to the pressure of the agency.

Archer delivered an express mail package to me in my office after school. I put it with the stack of mail I hadn't had time to address due to some sketchy cases on my desk that needed my attention more than the mail.

Stacy had yet to grace us with her presence today, which wasn't unusual. She preferred late nights, which resulted in her arriving in the late mornings or early afternoons to vacuum and dust the house. And today, Alessandra had a meeting at the pack clubhouse, so I was alone with Archer for the afternoon.

The sound of a car outside didn't fully register until Archer knocked on the door and stepped into the office again.

"Um, Dad, you have company."

I glanced up and looked beyond Archer.

My heart dropped, and I quickly schooled my features, letting only the surprise at seeing

Terrance Winters through. My mouth dried as he strolled into my office with an air about him that set my teeth on edge. I turned my attention to Archer.

"Weren't you heading to your friends after you got the mail?" I didn't want him here just in case things went south.

"I think he should stay. I'm here to see if your young ones are interested in a career in the Monster Defense Agency." He smiled, but there was tension behind it.

I leaned back in my wheelchair and studied Terrance. "Why aren't you discussing this with my wife? She is the alpha of this pack."

"What does the agency do?" Archer lingered by the door. He wasn't even a teenager yet, and I did not want him having ideas about working for this man. Not after everything Robert had told me.

I shot a sharp glare in his direction. "You've kept your friend long enough." I didn't mean for it to come out in a snap, but I also didn't want him hanging around. I glanced at the clock. "While you're at it, let the housekeeper know we have company, and she doesn't need to come by today."

His eyes widened a fraction, but not enough for anyone who didn't know the kid to suspect anything. Even though he didn't know Rosie's background, the mere fact I didn't want him to hang back for this conversation or her to barge in on it conveyed the need for privacy.

"Sure," he said after a beat.

I waved him away and then turned back to Terrance. "Now, I should call Alessandra."

"I think we can have this conversation without your wife."

I detected the condescending nature of his tone. As if a woman couldn't be an alpha. It irked me. "If it has to do with the pack…"

Terrance lifted his hand, stopping me. "It's more about the council rather than the pack." He took a seat in the chair facing my desk.

I waited in silence, unnerved by this visit already.

"I'd like to see if any of the packs would be interested in agency jobs."

"The council is not your recruiter." I stared him down. He couldn't shift, so I was in no danger of that type of attack, but I had my hand on the gun attached to my wheelchair.

He leaned forward. "I always thought an alliance between the werewolf council and the agency would be mutually beneficial." He studied his clasped fingers before raising his gaze, and my bullshit meter went into overdrive.

"If there had been an alliance, I don't think my brother would have strayed so far from doing what's right."

I narrowed my eyes at him, letting my skepticism bleed through. "And why didn't you have an alliance with your brother?"

His smile wasn't the least bit pleasant. It looked as if he had bitten into a sour lemon. "My brother wanted control of everything and that would have pushed me to the back of the pack. The agency is my domain, and I did not wish to give that up."

I cocked an eyebrow. "Then you will understand why I must decline."

He slowly sat back, perhaps realizing how much of his hand he just showed me in that little admission. "You don't trust me."

It wasn't a question. I stared him down. "You have the same blood in your veins as your brother, and he was a monster."

"Yes, he was. But I am not Ken. Besides, haven't I proved that over the last eleven years?" He held his hands out in faux innocence.

I sighed and wondered if I hadn't had a conversation with Robert, would I be considering this offer right now?

"I don't know that I'll ever fully trust anyone in your family." I kept his gaze and took a breath. "But that isn't why I would prefer to keep the organizations separate."

His eyebrow cocked as he waited for the rest of my explanation.

"We have our pack rules and, from what I understand, the agency is intertwined with our government. I'd prefer not to have government oversight on pack life. Humans don't understand our hierarchies or our laws." I gave him a tight smile. "Perhaps in another fifteen or twenty years, when there is more global acceptance of shifters, I may feel differently. But at this juncture, I really must decline your offer of access to the packs associated directly with the council."

His neck reddened, as if the bite of anger lived in his blood. I couldn't smell it, but he was always good at hiding his emotions. "Perhaps we can talk again when the pains of the past are truly put behind us."

I inclined my head in a slow nod, not really committing to anything that would put my constituents in danger. "Will I see you at the summit this year?"

"I may make an appearance if my schedule allows. Otherwise, I'll send Robert Young in my stead like I have for the past couple of years."

I pushed away from the desk and rolled out to the side of it. "I can show you out." I waved toward the door, waiting for him to step in front of me. I did not want this man at my back.

I followed him to the front door.

"Until the summit." He nodded and walked out the door to the waiting car. A driver opened the back door for Terrance and then hurried into the front seat.

I lifted my hand in a wave and watched until they were out of sight. The tightness in my chest abated enough for me to take a deep breath. And it was only then that I looked toward the garage.

The curtain twitched, and I saw a glimpse of Stacy staring out of the small crack. Our eyes met, and I gave her a thumbs-up, even though I wasn't settled at all by the visit.

Then I rolled back into my office and just stared at the paperwork in front of me without seeing what it was.

Terrance Winters had never set foot in this house before. The summit was always held at the town hall, where there was more than enough room to house all the alphas for all the packs who had a vote for the legislation we put forth. So, how did he get our private address? A shiver stalked down my spine.

A clearing of a throat made me jump, and I reached for my gun. At the sight of Stacy at the door, I exhaled long and loud and slouched in the chair.

"The agency?" she said with a voice drenched in dread. It matched the shaking in her hands and the fearful frown etched into her lips.

"Yes. But I'm not sure if this was a fishing expedition or some unspoken warning." I dropped my gaze to the express pouch. The source address registered and I snagged it out of the mail pile. With a rip of the seal, I dumped the contents on my desk.

"Is that what I think it is?" Her eyes filled with hope.

I nearly laughed at how damn thorough my contact was. Not only did he have a license in Rosie Beeswich's name, he had a passport with stamps in it, a birth certificate, and a Social Security number, along with a few wallet-size photos of her as a college graduate. Then there was a professional photo and dossier along with a work history list...even a couple of actual written recommendations for her maid work. And every one of the work history numbers would result in a glowing review of her work.

I gathered the documents and stretched my hand out. "Miss. Rosie Beeswich, it looks like you are free to go home to—" I glanced at the license on the top of the pile. "New Orleans whenever you'd like."

The smile she shined on me as she plucked the documents from my hand radiated through the room. She shuffled through the papers. When she looked up at me, the reality of the situation hit.

"It's been nice having a clean house," I said.

Her smile faded. "I owe you my life."

I laughed. "No, you paid your dues already. Cleaning up after Archer and me can't have been easy."

"You paid me for that. You hid me from that monster, gave me a roof and a job, and now this." She waved the papers. "I don't know if I'll ever be able to repay you and your wife."

My lips twitched into what I hoped was a smile. "Pay it forward. Help someone in need when you can, and that will be enough."

She pressed her new legal documents to her chest. "I will, Mr. Blaez. I promise I will never forget you."

"Will that be far enough away to mask your magical signature?" The after thought dropped before I could catch it.

"If it isn't, I can always go on a cruise around the world and just disappear on the other side of the globe." She smiled. "Besides, New Orleans is a hotbed of supernatural activity. It's one of the few places in the world that magic is so intertwined that the agency cannot differentiate, even with boots on the ground."

I had hoped that was the case, especially when my contact asked if that would be acceptable.

"I'll just pack up and be on my way."

"Do you have enough money?" I reached for the side drawer of my desk.

"I've kept most of the pay you've given me. It's more than enough for a bus ticket."

I reached into the metal cash container and pulled out a few bills, offering them to her, but she shook her head.

"You've done enough. Once I get there, I can find work easily with these recommendations." She waved at the documents.

"Take care." I didn't offer any other platitudes. This was always meant to be temporary.

She gave me a curt nod and spun on her heel, but not before I caught the sheen in her eyes.

I was going to miss her presence and her help around the house just as much as Alessandra. I might actually have to look into the maid service and hire one now that we'd had a taste of it for the last couple of months.

At least until I got another meeting request from Robert Young.

CHAPTER 9

MY PHONE DINGED, AND I glanced at the text from an unknown number. The same meeting place as before, with a date and time, blinked on the screen. I glanced across the dinner table at Alessandra and put my silverware down. I had just enough time to get there if I left right now.

"It seems a council member wants to discuss our latest case," I said.

Alessandra cocked her head with a look that screamed *'really?'*. The council never bothered me after work hours. It was an unwritten rule we all had. Unless it was a dire life-and-death emergency, it wasn't done during what we all considered family time.

"They want me to meet them down at the coffee shop near the strip mall with that jewelry store you like." I waved the screen at her, then pocketed my phone and rolled out from the table.

I moved toward the door and stopped by Alessandra's chair. I showed her the text, and her brow creased. It had been over a year since Stacy had left and I hadn't heard a thing from Robert. It looked like we were going to have another house guest, but this time, at least I had the network in place to get documentation much quicker than before.

"Be careful," she whispered.

Archer looked up from his phone and stared at the two of us. "Why would Dad need to be careful?"

"He's driving at night," Alessandra said without missing a beat.

I adored her quick thinking under the gun. Her ability to create a believable statement under duress was probably as sharp as mine.

"Oh." He went back to whatever game he was playing on his phone.

Alessandra gave me a peck on the cheek, and I rolled out of the house. From the ask on the text, I had a feeling this was another rescue operation. We hadn't talked since he dropped Stacy off, and he did not know that Terrance had swung by before Stacy left us.

I needed to let him know that happened. Terrance had never set foot in our territory without a formal invitation, and he certainly had never been to my house before. I pulled into the parking lot next to the coffee shop, but before I could get my wheelchair out of the car, the back passenger door opened, and Robert dropped into the seat.

"Drive," he said as he lay huffing on the seat.

I swung the wheelchair back into the car and closed my door before I backed out. "Where am I going?" I asked, trying to ignore the scent of blood coming from the back seat.

Fabric tore, and then the familiar pant of a wolf came from the space. A low whine escaped.

I sighed. "I wish like hell I could shift and heal my back, but my spine severed, and no shift will fix that. Believe me, I've tried." Werewolf shifting usually helped heal wounds. But in my case, with the severed spine from my accident, along with being stretched to almost being torn in half, even shifting, could not repair that catastrophic damage. I glanced in the rearview mirror and caught Robert's blue eyes surrounded by jet-black fur. "I know it hurts, but by the time you shift back, you'll be whole again."

His slow nod acknowledged my ramblings.

"Do you want me to take you to my house?"

He growled.

"A no then. Okay. So, I'll just drive around until you shift back and are ready to talk." I let the silence fill the car. I flipped on the radio and tuned into a rock station. I sang along while I drove in circles, watching behind me to make sure we weren't being followed.

Finally, a groan came from the back seat.

I shut off the music and pulled over in a quiet cul-de-sac. "What the fuck?" I turned toward the back of the car.

Robert slumped against the passenger door. "I was double-crossed."

My chest constricted, and Terrance's meeting jumped to the forefront of my mind. "Do they know I'm your contact?"

"No. And I killed him before he could report on his location. Thankfully, I destroyed his tracking before I left the city." He wiped his face. "And now I'm going to have to sacrifice my son to the organization in order to throw off suspicion."

He closed his eyes and leaned against the window.

I blinked and swallowed hard. "What do you mean, sacrifice?"

"I'm going to have to insist he go to the Monster Defense Academy and follow the same path to damnation that I've had to walk."

The devastation in his voice cut to my soul. "Did you know Terrance swung by just before Stacy took off?"

His eyes darkened. "I found out after the fact. Terrance wants control of the council, but he's not foolish enough to make a move that will put the agency at risk. Plus, I discouraged him from pushing further."

I didn't want to know how, but I was relieved he discouraged that maniac. "Thank you."

He nodded. "I've had to do some seriously shitty things to my kid over the years, but what's coming next is going to fuck up any chance of a relationship with him. But I will do anything I have to, so he survives."

"Why are you telling me this?"

"Because someone has to tell him I loved him if all this blows up in my face. I'm running a tightrope here, and it could fray under my feet at any moment."

I couldn't imagine alienating my child to keep them safe. It had to be a living nightmare. I laid back against the seat and rubbed my face, looking at him in the rearview mirror. "Where do we fall in this tightrope act?"

"You're my son's safety net." His eyes closed.

"How do I know you aren't playing me?" I challenged him. As much as I didn't want to entertain the thought, I had to be sure. After all, the organization he worked for wanted our council to offer our young to their agency. They wanted their hooks in us. If anything this wolf said was close to the truth, I had to protect our packs.

His eyes opened, and he stared at the rearview mirror. He didn't say anything for a few minutes. Then he whispered, "You don't. There isn't anything I can offer as proof that I'm not."

The fact he didn't press his alpha dominance on me said a lot. I knew he was just as powerful as Alessandra. If not more. And he could very well exercise that on me to coerce me, but he hadn't.

He rubbed his face. "I need to figure out a viable story about Greg. He was from another pack and Terrance asked me to get rid of him, since he screwed up an important job. So, Terrance might suspect I'm compromised."

"Did Greg know you had saved someone from the same fate?"

Robert shook his head. "I just asked him to go for a ride. No explanations, just like the others I've had to kill for valid reasons."

"You've embraced the job of assassination for the agency?"

Robert's sharp stare caught mine. "Yes. My hands are far from clean. I am very particular about who I choose to save. If I saved everyone who the agency put a hit on, I would have been in a grave a long time ago."

I shivered and wished I had my firearm. That was tucked safely in my chair at home in the garage. "And what if Terrance sends you on a job to take me out?"

"He wouldn't go after you. He'd go after your wife. The alpha of the pack. She's the one who appointed you to run the council." He cocked his head. "And you better make sure that if your son has the alpha mark, it isn't announced until he is out of school and on his way to a solid career."

I blinked, and my mouth dropped open before I could recover.

Robert chuckled from the back seat. "The agency knows how your pack alpha is chosen. It's something almost mystical and, from what I understand, centuries old. It has everything to

71

do with the original, and the fact your wife is from the original line hasn't been a secret."

My eyebrows rose. They didn't know whether Archer had the mark or not. I kept that to myself. This entire encounter seemed more of a threat than anything amicable.

"Are you threatening me?"

"No." The answer came quicker than expected. "You are the only ally I have. It behooves me to tell you what the agency knows about your family. Besides, the seer I went to told me I had one true ally in this mess and that he was bound to a mechanical chair." He waved at me.

Now my eyebrows felt as if they rose all the way to my hairline. "A seer?"

"Yeah. I found one outside the agency, and she gave me a private reading. I didn't want to believe a thing she said, but so far, she has been dead on. And if I don't somehow prevent my son from claiming his fated mate, I'll never get to see vengeance for my family. Apparently, she is the key, and I have to keep them apart. Otherwise, this entire world is fucking doomed."

Bitterness as thick as poisoned fog filled the car.

"And he has no choice but to join the agency." Robert's chin dropped to his chest. "So, whenever my time is up, I expect you to relay all this to my son. Hopefully, by that time, I am able to make amends with him.”

I put the car in gear and drove toward the coffee shop. “I assume you have the means to get out of our pack lands without an issue, correct?”

“Yes. And I apologize for the mess in your back seat. You’ll have to think of something to tell your wife that won’t alarm her.”

“My wife knows about our deal.”

His gaze shot to mine. “You told her?”

“I won’t ever lie to her. She’s my wife, and she’s my alpha. She owns my ass, as feeble as it is these days.”

“You may be in a wheelchair, but you aren’t feeble. You’re probably the most damned honorable son of a bitch I know.”

I snorted. “You know I killed humans out of vengeance, right?” I glanced back at him. “It’s why Leigh and I were wanted by the council.”

“The way I hear it, they had it coming.”

“It’s still against the law.” I wasn’t particularly proud of it, but after what they had done to Alessandra, there wasn’t a person on this green earth that could have stopped me from tearing their throats out.

"I would have tortured them slowly and reveled in their screams before I killed them."

Well, okay then. "Once I got over my rage, I knew I had to hide her until it all blew over. But I hadn't had a clue it was an actual trap. One way or another, the council wanted us dead, either by poison or by a farce trial." I flicked my gaze at him in the mirror.

Robert nodded. "Just be glad Terrance hadn't weaseled his way onto the council. Otherwise, it would have been the agency gunning for you."

I shivered as I pulled into the parking lot. I wouldn't have wanted the agency hunting us. The council was bad enough, but the agency trained for that kind of shit. "Was Stacy the only one you got out?"

"No. I got my partner out years ago. And I was able to help a couple of wolves, but not nearly as many as I wanted." He opened the door once I came to a stop. "I'll be in touch. I have a feeling there will be more to save in the coming years while the agency culls those who aren't militant about their rules."

"I'll be available any time you need me. And I'll see you at the next annual council meeting."

He nodded and shifted and then used his front paws to close the door. He was gone in an instant, and I prayed I would hear from him again. I didn't like being in the dark about the agency, even if I had to make a deal with the devil himself.

CHAPTER 10

HE HAD BEEN TRUE to his word. The next several years were packed with agency escapees. And Alessandra was just as invested in saving as many as possible. Wolves and witches made up most refugees, but occasionally we would get some other type of supernatural. My contacts became efficient in getting documentation for me and the longest time frame that they stayed with us was a month before I could send them on their way.

During those occasions, Robert and I had little time to chat. It was more of a handoff and then he'd be gone, as if he had never stepped into the shop. The only other time I saw him was at the annual council meetings, but there was no real chance to talk with so many ears around.

It was almost six years to the day from when I received that first text from Robert Young when I called a special annual meeting of the packs. This meeting had to do with the widespread use of silver by packs. Most just used it to lock up dangerous characters, but there were a few who needed to be called out for using it to keep members in line.

I knew this meeting would be a nightmare, but we had an important piece of legislation that needed to be voted on now, before things got more out of hand.

I rolled into the town hall with Alessandra by my side. Archer wasn't quite seventeen, so although we had talked with him about this new law, we didn't feel this was the right time to bring him into the fold of the council. Besides, he still didn't have that infamous mark of the leader of our pack.

Members milled about, and we took our places behind the council table. Minutes later, Robert walked in the door with a younger version of himself. Tension filled the air between the two of them, palatable enough to notice. Alessandra and I traded a glance as they strode across the floor toward us.

Robert smiled, but it didn't reach his eyes. He stopped in front of us, keeping my gaze for a second as if reminding me that no one else at the agency knew of his actions. Including his son. Then he said, "Chairman Blaez, Alpha Blaez, this is my son. Robert Young Jr." He waved at his look-alike. "Robby, this is Hunter and Alessandra Blaez."

Robby stuck his hand out, and his grip was firm.

"Robby has taken over as the alpha of the Allegany pack," Robert said.

Both our gazes jumped to him and then to his son. This news took me by surprise. We hadn't even received the notice of alpha change. Even though their pack was not one with the council's direct oversight, it usually was customary to notify us of the change.

"It was time for me to focus on the agency and make sure my pack had a good leader." Robert smiled and this time, it reached his eyes. "But I will still represent the agency at these meetings, while Robby represents the Allegany pack."

"Welcome." Alessandra hooked her arm into Robby's. "Let me introduce you to the other alphas." She steered him away, leaving me with his father without me having to suggest it to her.

Robert stepped around the table and stood next to me as we watched Alessandra lead him away. "He knows nothing," he said very softly.

"I got that."

"And he won't unless I am dead."

"Got that, too."

"He hates me."

I huffed. I could have told him that just from the animosity radiating from his son. But the pain in Robert's tone hit home. I wouldn't be able to deal with that kind of animosity aimed at me from Archer. "He'll understand someday."

"I hope so." He was quiet for a moment. "Terrance wants me to force Robby to marry his niece."

"And what of his fated mate?" I looked up at Robert, and his expression soured.

"She's his partner. If they cross the line, she dies, according to company policy."

"That's fucking barbaric," I muttered.

"The agency is fucking barbaric." He glanced around and cleared his throat.

Werewolves were known for their exceptional hearing, and even though we were speaking in hushed tones, anyone close by could make out what we were saying if they were tried.

"Have you read the newest bylaws up for vote today?" I asked in my normal tone and turned my attention to him fully. I had made certain that the use of silver in any manner with werewolves as a point of torture or containment was not allowed.

"Yes. The agency has some reservations but will comply with the majority vote." He gave me a look that told me they'd do whatever they damn well pleased despite whatever law was written today.

I wasn't sure the law would stand as it was spelled out, and I expected some modifications in this meeting, especially considering I had already received written notification against it.

It had the makings of a very spirited debate indeed. By the time we settled in our seats, the rumblings had begun. I grabbed the gavel that had been set out on the table and cleared my throat before I pounded it to get everyone's attention.

An unsettled silence fell over the room. I glanced to either side of me and the six alphas representing the council, including Alessandra. We had come to a consensus on the wording of the new law, but even that had taken longer than I had hoped. But as I looked out at the floor at the near hundred other packs represented, the animosity was louder than the hush.

"You all are aware of the prior council's legacy of torture and killing with silver." Rumblings continued among the alphas. "I witnessed one of our pack members dunked into a vat of boiling silver." Shudders ran through me as that vision surfaced again. I wasn't the only one in the room who reacted to that statement, either. Most of the alphas frowned, and some even bared their teeth. "I was supposed to be next, but my wife saved me." I glanced at Alessandra before launching into the meat of this gathering. "I have worked diligently with the alphas at this table to come up with a law regarding the use of silver for years. And you were all sent the final agreed-upon version."

"And if we don't agree with that version?" The voice in the back came from the alpha of one of the southwestern packs.

"Then we discuss the points you have contention with, Jared." I called him out. Jared Thurman hadn't accepted my appointment to the council and had been contentious ever since. And any time a council member stepped down, he threw his name in the ring. Thankfully, he could never get enough votes to back him. He was just as twisted as Winters had been and wanted the power of a council seat.

He weaved his way through the crowd, emitting a low growl as he approached the table where we sat. "You are purposely sabotaging our ability to keep our pack in line." He leaned on the table, staring down at me.

If only I could stand, I would have towered over him. Alessandra let out a growl, and I shot my hand out for her to stop. I wasn't an alpha like the rest of the room, but I had to stand my ground in order to gain their continued respect.

I let out a warning growl and leaned forward. "You use silver to keep your pack in line?"

The mood in the room instantly turned as I twisted his words against him. Snarls erupted behind Jared. No alpha here needed outside torture instruments to do that. I knew the core of their argument against the law as written was based on being able to cage those who perpetrated more serious crimes rather than the clause for keeping members in line.

He blinked as if he realized what had just come out of his mouth. And then his glare pinned on me. His shift was quick, but my draw was faster. I pointed my gun at the wolf snarling at me from the other side of the table. If he had launched, he would already be dead.

"I pack silver bullets in this gun." Thankfully, my hand remained steady as I stared down the alpha. Even if the bullets weren't silver, a headshot would still kill. But this way, if I missed a major organ, the silver poisoning would do the job, except it would be a hell of a lot more painful.

"Stand down." The order settled over the room, and most of the alphas actually lowered their heads in obedience under the power of the order.

The only alpha in the room who wasn't impacted by the decree was my wife. She kept her gaze on the alpha who had issued the order. I fought against the command and nearly lowered the gun, but I only obeyed *my* alpha's orders. When she used her alpha influence in these meetings, it had the same effect on the others.

Robby Young stepped away from his father's side. The alpha energy coming from him was just as powerful as my wife's. I'd wager it was more powerful than his father's, as well.

Jared cowered under the command.

I slowly lowered my gun to the table but kept my hand on it just in case Jared decided he wanted to kill me despite the Allegany alpha's show of dominance.

"Explain," Robby demanded of Jared as he towered over him. The fury in his eyes matched a majority of the wolves in the room.

I didn't interrupt, either. I wanted to see what this alpha was made of.

Jared shifted and turned on Robby Young. "Who the fuck are you?"

Robby Young smiled in a way that unsettled me. "I'm the alpha of the Allegany pack and an agent for the Monster Defense Agency."

I traded a glance with his father from across the room, but Robert Senior didn't flinch. He just crossed his arms and watched the show like the rest of the alphas in the room.

Jared spit on his shoes.

Robby's reaction was instantaneous. His hand shot out and clasped around Jared's neck, surprising all of us. When he pulled him close to his face, the growl in his throat was on the edge of deadly.

Jared clawed at his arm, but Robby held fast.

"Anyone using silver to punish pack members should be sentenced to death. It's one thing to lock up dangerous wolves in a cell made of silver, but that's not the same as what you are insinuating."

I respected Robby Young even more than I did his father. He held the righteousness that a protective alpha should. I glanced at Alessandra, and she gave me a sideways look, confirming her approval as well.

"Stand down," she commanded.

Robby slid his glare in her direction.

"This council will investigate and render judgment if need be. But thank you for your support." She smiled in a way that announced her agreement.

Robby tossed Jared away and made his way back to stand by his father. But his interruption did not ease the tensions in the room.

"Council, if I may approach," the alpha from the northwestern pack asked.

I nodded. This alpha was blonde and built like a bombshell. "Clara." I bowed my head to her as she stepped a respectable distance from the table.

"Hunter." She used the nickname everyone had called me since I was little. Only Alessandra called me by my real name. "Council." She showed her respect with the same tilt of her head. "I think I speak for a majority here when I state we do not have an issue with the torture and terrorizing piece of your legislation. What we have issue with is not being able to imprison felons and dangers to our society in silver cells."

I leaned back in my chair. This was the one thing we internally fought over, but eventually, my logical argument won. "Define cell."

"A standard jail cell, similar to the size of those found in human jails."

My lip twitched, and I glanced at the council surrounding me. Clara had just confirmed the definition I was hoping for, because just saying a cell was not enough. Some would consider a six-by-six cell enough, but most werewolves could be taller than six feet, thus a six-by-six cell wouldn't be enough to be comfortable without the threat of burning skin on the silver.

"I would concede to amending the legislation to include jail cells of no less than eighty square feet that have bars of silver to imprison those who commit serious crimes and are dangerous to the pack and society. But there must be proof of the crimes enough to convict in a court of law in order for you to jail any offender."

The room exploded in conversation. I waited to hear the consensus. I already knew what the council alphas at the table thought. This was what we had dared to hope for. We knew it would be more readily accepted if the alphas thought they put it on the table instead of us dictating the rules, but I wasn't about to leave the torture clause to the committee. I wouldn't bend on that one despite the heated debates we had on the matter.

Clara turned to the rest of the alphas and engaged in their conversation. After a few minutes, she turned back to us. "We accept those changes."

I nodded and glanced at the alphas surrounding me. "Council members, all in favor of adding the language to the legislation?"

"Aye." Every one of them raised their hand.

I looked at the room. "With a unanimous vote from the council, I turn it to you to vote. All in favor?"

Everyone but Jared raised their hands.

"Opposed?"

Jared slowly raised his hand.

I glanced at the lone hand raised. "Let the record show one opposed. Majority rules. As such, this legislation passes." I hit the gavel on the table and stowed my gun back in the holster on the inside of my chair armrest. "Is there any new business that we'd like to discuss?"

All eyes turned to Jared.

Alessandra cleared her throat. "What are you doing with silver to keep your pack in line?" she asked Jared directly.

His growl filled the space. "None of your fucking business."

I sighed and nodded to Kyle, the alpha from western Texas who had been on the council as long as we had. He was one of our first allies after the original council perished. He rose and crossed to the side door. He stopped and faced us with his hand on the knob.

"Last chance to come clean, Jared." I turned my stare in his direction.

"I should have torn your throat out the first time we met," he growled at me.

Alessandra's menacing growl filled the space, and she launched over the table, shifting in mid-flight. Her powerful jaws clamped down on his human throat, snapping closed. Jared's head hit the floor and rolled to the middle of the room. His death was as swift and violent as I had ever seen her deliver.

She shifted back and stood tall in all her naked glory. The tattoo on her abdomen glowed with her power. But in case the group had any qualms about Jared's death, I gave Kyle the signal, and he opened the door.

Three men and one woman stepped in the room. All of them had silver burns on their cheeks and their arms. The brand on the woman's shoulder actually made my stomach roll.

Jared's execution was warranted. Although I wish I had shot him with a silver bullet instead of having my wife kill him in such a vicious display. But I suppose her actions reinstated her post as the head of all of us in the room. She even made Robby's cheeks dull, and he was probably the only alpha in this room who could challenge her.

Sharon, the alpha next to Alessandra, handed her a bathrobe as I concluded the meeting. With Jared's body still marring the floor, we skirted around the blood and gore and headed toward the door and the fresh evening air.

At least it was the bastard I had been researching who bit it. This entire meeting was more about posturing than legislation. And we pulled it off with no one else being harmed.

I was glad that my goal for this meeting had been addressed before blood flew. That didn't always happen at these things. Too many alphas in a room were bound to launch tensions beyond the brink.

That was one of the few reasons I hated being on the council. It put a target on our backs.

CHAPTER 11

THE YEAR WENT BY with no tensions, but we had a few transient refugees from Robert. Archer had just started his senior year in the pack high school and was doing well in all his classes, and we had visited a few prospective colleges over the summer months.

On this cool fall afternoon, I sat in my office, going over the latest documents for the next annual council meeting. Archer slid inside and took the seat across from the desk. He rarely bothered me in my office after school, but right now, his anxiety pelted me hard enough that I stopped reading in the middle of the case instead of finishing before I gave him my attention.

"Everything okay?" I closed the case folder I had been reading.

He laughed and looked at his hands. "Well, it depends on your viewpoint."

I raised an eyebrow. "What is it?"

"Well, Cheryl's pregnant."

My brain stalled. I blinked at him. I wasn't sure I heard right. "What?"

"I didn't want to tell Mom."

He had the sense to look uncomfortable, but it wasn't enough to dull my building anger. "Why are you sleeping with her? You aren't even eighteen!"

He rolled his eyes at me. "We've been together since freshman year."

"Do her parents know?" My entire mind went into damage control mode. Hopefully, the due date would be after graduation, but it still meant their futures were now limited. The idea of my son's potential being shot down because of an act of stupidity nearly made me lose my shit.

"Not yet. She's afraid to tell them." He picked at a hangnail.

"So, what? You expect us to tell them?" My question was filled with angry snark, and the fury just escalated when he raised a shoulder and dropped it in a half-assed shrug.

I sent out a silent request for my wife to come to my office because I mentally couldn't deal with this alone. Thankfully, the connection we had was stronger than most mates. She probably already knew I was pissed, but she usually assumed my aggravation was council related.

"What's up?" she asked from the doorway.

Archer glared at me. "You called Mom?"

"Yes." I waved at her while staring him down. "Go ahead."

Alessandra stepped into the office, and her concern radiated from her. She looked between the two of us as Archer shifted in the seat and stared at the ground. "What's going on?"

"Your son has something to say."

My phrasing caught her by surprise, and her eyebrows darted up. Normally, I referred to him as our son, unless I was furious. She crossed and took the seat next to him and covered his hand. "What is it, honey?"

He pinched his lips together and inhaled loudly. "Cheryl's pregnant."

She pulled her hands away and leaned back in the chair. Disappointment etched into her face, pulling her lips down, and the sickly sweet scent of it drifted around her. "Do they not teach you about protection in school?" The edge in her voice matched the anger rubbing my skin raw.

"It was only one time," he protested with a whine.

"That's all it takes." I would not fall for this *pitiful me* act.

Alessandra nodded. "What are you going to do about it?" She crossed her arms.

"I-I don't know," he stuttered, looking between the two of us.

"This isn't our mess to clean up, Archer," I said.

He looked utterly lost, and his eyes darted around in panic. I remembered feeling overwhelmed by the thought of a child, and Alessandra and I had been living together at the time. We were not in high school, although she had been in college when our lives turned upside down because of Winters and his schemes.

"Well, you better start figuring out a plan," Alessandra said.

Archer wasn't reacting well to our less than compassionate response. His frantic blinking nearly made me laugh, but the subject at hand was as far from funny as it got in parenting. When Alessandra told me I was going to be a father, I had literally freaked out. Just putting myself back in those shoes humbled me. It also quieted the anger rioting in my blood a fraction.

"What does Cheryl want to do?" I tried to keep all the frustration still present from leaking into my voice.

His wide eyes caught mine. "She doesn't want an abortion." He swallowed hard. "And neither do I."

I should have expected that from our child. We believed life was a gift and fought diligently to make sure everyone else had fair treatment. Of course, we had limits and laws that forfeit life when broken. But we believed in the sanctity of life, so his decision to not abort a child made sense.

"Okay," Alessandra said, stretching the word out.

"So, we are back to the question of what are you going to do?" I piped in when he didn't take Alessandra's baited question.

He picked at his hangnail. "I was thinking of that Monster Defense Academy."

"Absolutely not," I said at the same time as Alessandra's snarling, "No."

Archer's eyes widened as he stared at me. "Why not?"

"First of all, the academy does not pay. Second, the agency is a deplorable institution, and I will not have you under their thumb." I leaned forward. "Plus, it isn't something that you bring a child into. Not when your life is in danger, and you could drag that shit home with you."

He made some disrespectful noise, as if I didn't know what I was talking about.

"What happens to you if a vampire you're hunting finds your home and kills everyone you love? Huh?"

"That doesn't happen," he scoffed at me.

"Yes. It does. I know at least a half a dozen people who have suffered that fate." I bit my tongue on telling him he'd met a few as well. I heard some of their stories while he was off at school and I was getting their fake identifications in place. "Vampires, rogues, soul eaters, ghouls. You name it, once you hunt it, you become a target. Is that what you want for your family?"

"But I thought..." He trailed off.

"You thought what?" I stared him down, and Alessandra let me lead this conversation. "That the agency protects their people?" I laughed, but there was no trace of humor in it.

"Well, yeah. That's what they said at school."

Alessandra growled in her seat. "The Monster Defense Agency has been in your school?"

"Yeah." He glanced at her and then back at me. "On career day."

"Shifters have been on our pack lands?" Her clipped question agreed with the red now filling her face.

He shook his head. "They were human, not shifters."

"Choose something else," I said through clenched teeth.

"You can't stop me!" he yelled and stood.

"Sit down," Alessandra snarled in her alpha tone.

Archer sat so quickly, I almost smirked.

"You cannot ever consider the Monster Defense Agency as a prospective future. That is a direct order from your alpha." Her power even made me want to curl in on myself.

Archer's shoulders rounded, and he stared at the ground. "Then make me alpha."

Alessandra stared at him for at least three solid beats of my heart. "I can't. You do not carry the mark."

It wasn't something she could pass down from generation to generation, like Robert could do with his son. Our pack required the mark of the alpha to be present. Alessandra contained the authority of the alpha, and after her father disappeared, we assumed she was the proper alpha just by her incredible power. However, it wasn't until that mark appeared that she was recognized by the elders in the pack.

Unfortunately, Archer did not develop that power in puberty like we had hoped.

"Then what the hell am I going to do?"

His outburst set my teeth on edge, and I clenched my jaw.

"Get a real job, marry that girl, and raise that child the best you can. Understand?" My wolf shot to the surface, and I closed my eyes, stuffing him back in the cage that was my broken body.

"But she's expecting me to become the alpha," he whined.

"You are going to need to manage her expectations." Alessandra stared him down.

"But Mom..."

"I love you with everything I am, but you do not have the mark. I cannot hand the pack to someone without the mark. It just isn't the way our pack works."

At least she didn't tell him he didn't have the authority of an alpha. That's a confidence killer.

"Fine." He chewed on his lip for a moment. "She wants me with her when we tell her parents."

"Good luck with that," Alessandra said under her breath.

"Can you be there with us?" He wasn't looking at his mother.

I pointed to my chest, and Archer nodded. "Why, so you can hide behind the cripple when her father launches to kill you?"

"N-n-no."

His stuttering reaction gave me pause. "Then why?"

"Because you're the calmest wolf in the pack. And Mom will just issue an order to sit and deal with it. I don't want to piss them off more than they will already be."

"If he takes a swing at you, I can't stop him."

His gaze dropped to my sidearm.

I huffed. "I only pull that if I intend to use it. Besides, you deserve a punch for sleeping with her with no protection or thought of either of your futures."

"You really don't want me there?" Alessandra asked.

Archer shook his head. "I love you, Mom. But you can be scary if someone even looks at us wrong."

He wasn't incorrect. And when Alessandra turned her attention to me, I shrugged. My mind went to the last council meeting where blood was spilled. Alessandra had been the one to react.

If Cheryl's father launched at Archer while she was in the room, she wouldn't be able to sit and allow him harm. It just was not in her to allow either of us to get hurt. Not since I nearly died at the hands of our enemies.

CHAPTER 12

THE CARSON'S WERE MID-LEVEL pack members; the moment I rolled into the local pub with Archer, they stood as if I were some visiting dignitary. It made me uncomfortable, as if they were expecting great things from the relationship between our son and their daughter.

"George, Tabitha," I said as I rolled to the table they sat at. I had chosen this place because it was rather empty for the afternoon, plus it had a handicap ramp. I did not want to raise this issue in either of our homes.

I didn't expect violence, but I still had my side arm on the chair. I never went anywhere without it because it was my best bet at surviving an attack.

"Hunter," they both said and dipped their heads.

"To what do we owe this pleasure?" Tabitha added as they sat down.

I pulled to the head of the table. Archer and Cheryl sat to my right while George and Tabitha were to my left. I took a breath and glanced at the two kids. Neither of them would meet my gaze. From their lack of speaking up, it seemed they were letting me lead this conversation. I was not willing to let them off the hook.

"Our children have something to say," I said.

Archer sent me a sideways glare. Cheryl didn't even look up from the menu that sat before her, but she stiffened in the seat next to Archer.

Archer cleared his throat and took Cheryl's hand in his. "I'd like to marry your daughter."

My eyebrow rose, and I kept my reaction neutral, while the excited gasps from the Carsons made my center tighten in frustration.

Archer peeked up at Mr. and Mrs. Carson, and then his gaze darted to me.

"Oh, we can plan such a grand affair for the spring after graduation." Tabitha almost bounced out of her seat at the thought.

"Well, we'd like to do it as soon as possible," Archer said. "Right, hon?" he asked Cheryl.

"Yes. I'd like to marry Archer next weekend." She looked up and straightened her spine.

The Carsons traded a glance before they looked at me. The gears in their head were spinning, and I wasn't giving them any indication of my dark mood. I hadn't been privy to this plan, either, and the fact I wasn't smiling also must have been a factor, because finally George's eyes narrowed at my son.

"Why the hurry?" he asked, but it came out in more of a growl.

"Because I'm pregnant with Archer's child." Cheryl's voice seemed steady, the bead of sweat at her temple belied her nerves.

Tabitha just stared at the two teenagers with her mouth open. All her dreams of a grand wedding fizzled into palpable anger.

George shot to his feet. "Why you..." he started and then launched over the table, shifting in the air. He slammed into Archer and both of them toppled over onto the ground.

This wasn't what I expected. Although I thought Archer needed to be punched for his lapse of judgment, I did not agree with a full-on beating, or worse. And the fury radiating in the small space was on par with murder. He was going to kill my son right in front of me, despite his wife's and daughter's frantic pleas.

The cock of my gun caught everyone's attention. George's wolf growled at Archer, but his eyes were now on me.

"If you so much as scratch my son with your damned teeth, I will shoot you." My words came out in a feral growl, accompanied by a deadly glare.

Silence filled the entire place. No one moved.

"Back off slowly and then take a seat, George." My voice carried my beta power. It wasn't as powerful as Alessandra's alpha, but I carried my own level of deterrent in order to keep the peace. I waited until he moved away, shifted back into human form, and took a seat in the buff.

A staff member ran over with a bathrobe for him. Most bars within pack lands had one or two on hand if things got out of control in the establishment. I gave her a nod and put my gun away. If my spine hadn't been severed, I would have shifted and stopped him before he even reached Archer.

I once had been a scary son of a bitch. Several elder pack members assumed I might actually be the one to get the mark, but I was never as strong as Alessandra. Even so, no one messed with me before the accident. Hell, this would have never happened had I not been in a wheelchair.

Once he was covered up, his gaze snapped at me. "You condone this?" He waved at the two teenagers now huddled together on the opposite side of the table, rattled by what had occurred.

"No. I do not condone this at all. What they did was stupid and reckless. But they did it all the same. It takes two people to make a child and from what I understand, this was a mutual screwup." I looked at Cheryl and got a nod in response before I met George's angry glare.

"I can't believe you put any blame on my daughter," Tabitha finally said after she recovered from the last few tense minutes.

"Mom, I wasn't forced into anything. Archer and I made the mutual decision. I wanted him just as much as he wanted me, so don't make this into more of an issue than it is." She took a breath. "We've known forever that this was it for us." She shrugged and then took a sip of her water. "It just means we'll be together earlier than planned."

I blinked at her calm demeanor in the face of her father's outburst.

"I love your daughter, Mr. Carson." He inspected his ripped shirt and the welts left in his chest before he met his future father-in-law's gaze. "We didn't intend for this to happen. And yes, it was reckless for us not to have had any protections in place—"

"You shouldn't be sleeping with my daughter!" His growl was back as he spoke over Archer.

"You two slept together before you were married." Cheryl fluttered her hand at her parents. "So do not judge us."

"We were not in high school," Tabitha scolded.

I watched this train wreck unfold and kept my comments to myself. I wasn't happy with the situation, but I understood their point of view.

How long had I pined for Alessandra?

I was a couple of years older than she was, so approaching her while she was in high school wouldn't have been cool. But Archer and Cheryl were the same age and basically had been together for their entire high school tenure.

"But where will you live? What will you do about school? How will you afford a child?" Her mother fired questions without giving them a break to answer.

Archer finally lifted his hand, stopping the questions from continuing to barrel at him. "First, I get it. You're as pissed as my parents were, but we have a plan. We'd like to live in the apartment above the garage at my folks' for now."

He glanced at me, but I didn't confirm or deny that as an option. I wasn't sure that was available, especially considering that was my hiding place for Robert's agency refugees. I would have to think about what we'd do in the event we had any more before the kid could get on his feet and get out of our house.

"The baby isn't due until June, so we'll graduate before the baby comes." He glanced at Cheryl, and she gave him a nervous smile. "We'll get jobs. One of us first shift and the other either second or third depending on if there is a crossover of hours, and we'll see if we can find online degrees in the subjects that interest us. It might take us longer to get a degree, but we'll be able to do it while taking care of the baby."

My eyebrow rose at his semi-thorough explanation. He had just told me about this yesterday, so either he came up with this plan pretty damn fast, or he and Cheryl had talked about what to do before he told me and was waiting for an audience to share their plan.

Both their gazes jumped from her parents to me and back. I kept my emotions in check and did not show that I was surprised. Her father's anger still stunk up the air like a batch of burned toast, but at least he was no longer assaulting my kid.

"So, will you give us permission to marry next weekend?" Cheryl asked her parents.

They looked at me for an answer, but it wasn't my decision. I had already given my son an ultimatum when he told me, and it looked like he had taken it to heart. "It's not my decision," I said after too long a silence.

"We'd like you to be at the wedding." Cheryl's voice was nearly a whisper, but it caught her father's entire attention.

"You should have thought of that before you opened your legs. You are a disgrace. Consider yourself disowned," George snapped and grabbed his wife's hand, pulling her to her feet along with him as he stood. He looked at me. "She's your problem now."

They marched out of the restaurant like a pair of angry toddlers, leaving me with my son and his pregnant girlfriend.

"Maybe we should have brought your mother," I muttered under my breath and focused on the teenagers. Archer's eyes were almost as wide as his slack mouth. Cheryl's chin trembled as the door closed behind her parents. Her gaze jumped to mine, and her panic soiled the air with a bitter tinge.

Archer put his arm around Cheryl, pulling her close and then met my gaze. "What now?"

I sighed. "It looks like we need to get the guest room ready."

"What about the apartment over the garage?"

"We built that for visiting dignitaries. Not for you to shack up in while you both are in high school." Besides, I had to talk to Alessandra before I made that kind of decision. "We need to get your mother to go to Cheryl's house to grab whatever she needs in the way of clothing, along with her schoolbooks."

They nodded.

Before I rolled away from the table, I pulled out a twenty and left it under the saltshaker for the trouble we caused, even though we hadn't ordered anything yet. The staff had kept their distance while the discussion occurred. They probably read the emotions of all parties and made the wise decision not to interfere with the conversation. Other than delivering the bathrobe, they had been scarce.

"Come on, you two. You have to deliver the news of how this went to your mother. And I expect she will be pissed."

CHAPTER 13

"WHAT HAPPENED?" ALESSANDRA ASKED the moment she got a look at who was walking through the door.

I rolled into the house after Archer and Cheryl. "It looks like we will have a long-term houseguest." I cut my gaze to Cheryl to give her a chance to digest that. "Archer, set Cheryl up in the guest room while I talk to your mother."

Archer opened his mouth and then shut it before he nodded.

I am glad he didn't argue with me. I wasn't in the mood to deal with his attitude right now. And I did not want to talk to Alessandra where he could hear. I rolled into my soundproof office. A moment later, she followed and closed the door.

"What happened?"

I rubbed my face. "Her father attacked him. It wasn't a punch. He shifted and went for Archer's throat. I had to pull my gun and threaten to shoot his ass if he harmed my son."

Her mouth dropped open.

"I'm actually glad I can't shift into a functioning wolf. If I could, her father would have died on the spot." I met her gaze. "And it is good you weren't there for the same reason."

"But what is she doing here?"

"They disowned her and said she's our problem now." I shook my head as I tapped my fingers on the arms of the chair. It was my nervous tendency since I couldn't pace the room. "And apparently, they are getting married this coming weekend."

Alessandra made a noise like a squeak.

"And he thinks they can stay in the apartment over the garage."

Her mouth popped closed. "That's for…"

"No shit. I couldn't very well say that out loud, either. So, it looks like either we have Robert's refugees stay in the house with us, or we have Archer and Cheryl in here along with a baby."

She chewed her bottom lip. "Both have their drawbacks. I'm not all that thrilled about waking throughout the night, but I'd rather have my son under our roof than a stranger."

I exhaled a breath I hadn't realized I was holding. She nailed my discomfort. Although I had become less wary of the refugees fed through this channel, I still wasn't comfortable sharing space with them on a regular basis.

"What do we tell Archer?"

"I will talk to him," Alessandra said. "And don't worry, I'll explain that the space over the garage is for traveling dignitaries from other packs and for those in transition who need a roof over their head. It isn't a big enough space for a child. There isn't a second bedroom over there. But they can take over the guest room once they are married and we can turn Archer's room into a nursery."

I tilted my head at the excitement finding its way into her tone. "Are you going soft on me?"

She laughed. "She's carrying our grandchild, Jake."

"I know." And despite being angry at my son and his hormones, I found myself just as enamored with the idea of a grandchild as my wife.

"We need to make it crystal clear that we" — she pointed between us—"are not raising their children for them."

I couldn't have agreed more with her statement. I just grinned instead of commenting.

CHAPTER 14

SPRING STROLLED IN LIKE a hurricane and with it came another meeting with Robert.

I arrived at the coffee shop and settled at a table with my drink, just waiting for Robert. I glanced at my watch. He was late, and I wondered whether he had another incident. Instead of heading outside, I sipped the hot drink and pondered what lies I would have to tell my son and daughter-in-law. At least they still had school for another couple of months.

My nerves prickled, and then the bell over the shop door jangled. A man that I could only describe as cagey preceded Robert into the shop. He looked jumpier than a junkie shooting up on the street. They crossed to the counter and put in their order while I continued to study them. All my internal alarms clanged like a tornado siren.

Thankfully, this coffeehouse was run by humans and not pack members.

When they sat down at the table with me, I had to fight not to recoil. Not only were my nerves on edge, but this close, my senses stung, making my hackles rise. If I were in wolf form, everyone would have known I was fighting going on the attack. Robert didn't look affected by this man's scent. I stared him down and cocked my head.

Usually, I greeted him with a smile. Not this time.

"I have a pregnant teenager in my home, and you want me to bring this into my house?" I hissed and waved at the stranger. "Alessandra will attack on instinct alone."

Robert hung his head. "John has done nothing against the law, yet the agency saw fit to eliminate him." He met my gaze. "I don't condone that. Even if he is a hybrid witch with a mix of demon blood."

"How did he get on your radar?" I crossed my arms.

"They killed my son, and I foolishly resurrected him, thinking it would be okay," John breathed.

"A necromancer," I hissed under my breath and visibly shivered. Necromancers were abominations, and the things they brought back were worse.

"I had to try," he added. "Even though I logically knew what came back to life would never be my son, I thought..." John wiped his face. "I put him down right before my house was raided by the agency."

I closed my eyes and pinched the bridge of my nose.

"I found him with the remains of his son." Robert's gaze met mine. We both knew what we would do for our children. "I hid him and then cleared the house. I got him in my trunk with no one noticing and then burned the house to the ground."

The explanation didn't help. I couldn't hide his stench or the danger response it evoked. Thankfully, this shop was on the outskirts of pack lands; otherwise, there would have been a bloodbath the moment John stepped out of Robert's car. "If I wasn't chained to this wheelchair, I would have attacked the moment he walked in the door. I cannot see Leigh being any different."

"Robert assured me I wouldn't be put in danger." John looked between the two of us.

"Your smell set me off. Can you mask it?"

"Not without using magic, and from what Robert told me, my magical signature is unique."

"Fuck." I pulled out my phone and dialed Alessandra. I put my finger up, silencing them both. "Hey, babe. Can you come down to the coffee shop?"

"What's wrong?"

I laughed a little. "I need your opinion before I agree."

Silence met my comment and then an exhale. "I'll be there in a half hour."

I disconnected the call and nodded toward the counter. "We might as well get some food because not only will Leigh be pissed off at having to come down here, she's likely to be hangry on top of that." I went to roll away from the table.

"I've got it. What will she want?" Robert stood and glanced at the menu.

I didn't need to look at the menu. I knew it by heart after all the visits here over the years. "The Philly cheesesteak. Make that two orders. I expected to eat at home, too."

Robert glanced at John.

"Make that three." He gave me a smile of commiseration.

"Four cheesesteaks." With a nod, he moved to the counter.

"My wife had a pretty volatile temper," John said as Robert put in the orders.

"What happened to her?" Usually, Robert's refugees had the same sad story. I really didn't want to hear another one, but we had to kill some time.

John tilted his head and stared at the table for a moment. His silver hair blocked my view of his face. "She turned me in, and I've been running ever since." He let out a sarcastic laugh. "Black magic is frowned upon in the agency, especially for an agent's spouse."

Robert slid into the seat across from me, and I gave him a pointed look. This person didn't seem innocent like the rest. I was about as comfortable with black magic as I was with necromancy.

"Your wife is no longer breathing." His statement hung on the air, and John slowly nodded. Robert pinned me with his gaze. "The black magic he is talking about was for me. It blocks seers in the agency from seeing anything beyond what I want them to."

My eyes widened, and Robert's protective instincts all fell into place. This man had sacrificed his relationship and his freedom for Robert.

"She set off the alarm, but didn't know what the magic was for. And John was bound to keep my secret." He glanced at John. "Which ended his relationship and nearly got him killed. Unfortunately, his son wasn't so lucky."

I wiped my face and shook off the feeling of emotional whiplash. I still wasn't comfortable with either of these men, but I would honor the agreement. I just needed Alessandra to not react to the stench and come up with some sort of story to tell our son and his wife. They could be just as triggered as I was.

And teenagers talk.

The server interrupted us by placing the four plates on the table. "Can I get you anything to drink?"

"Water would be good." I smiled up at her, hiding my discomfort.

As if on cue, the jangle of the door hitting the bell rang across the tiny space.

Alessandra froze on the spot and trembled. I met her gaze as she fought her wolf, and the alarm blazing in her eyes quirked the edge of my lips. My smile did nothing to quell her alpha vibe filling the shop.

Robert stiffened in the chair, and the fine hairs on his arms rose. He didn't even turn to acknowledge Alessandra; however, he waved his hand to the empty seat with the untouched plate in front of it.

Alessandra walked to the table as if her legs were made of wood and not flesh. The low growl in her throat got more pronounced the closer she got, and I already knew this probably would go to hell very quickly.

She stared at John across the table as she slowly lowered to the seat. The smell of her sandwich had her gaze dropping for a split second.

"I'm John. Your husband said I don't smell very appealing." He offered an apology smile and a shrug. "I mean no harm," he added before he took a bite of his food.

The high-pitched laugh that came from Alessandra made Robert twitch in his seat.

I took a bite of my food to stall whatever might fall out of my mouth.

"How am I supposed to hide him?" She stared at Robert. "No amount of air fresheners will dull that." She waved at John. "And it's not like we are on the outskirts of town like this place is. We are in the heart of our pack."

"He can't use his magic, and I don't know of any witches who can do that kind of wizardry without throwing up all manner of red flags," Robert said. "It's not ideal, but he needs to get out of the country as soon as possible." He turned his gaze on me. "Preferably a place that accepts more pagan-like religions where he could blend in."

Alessandra looked John up and down. "That would be fine if he was dark-skinned, but he's as white as my Irish uncle. He will stick out on most of the islands."

Robert and John snorted laughter.

"I'd prefer going somewhere that the agency has no reach," John said. "Somewhere easy to get lost."

"And where magic, particularly dark magic, is in abundance. I'd suggest Haiti, but there are so many issues happening there that I'd be concerned—"

"Haiti would be perfect," John interjected. "There's a lot of magic layering over that country, enough so that my wife mentioned more than once that the island has more power than most places, but nothing the agency could pinpoint."

I took a breath. "I can get you to New Orleans—"

Robert put his hand up and shook his head. "He needs to leave the country."

"Why?" Alessandra asked.

"Because there wasn't a body, and my boss has made it clear that the agency needs to find him and put him down before he disappears. New Orleans was one of the first places he tasked agents to look."

"That's all well and good, but it will take time to arrange." I took another bite. "And short of dousing him from head to toe in peppermint essential oil, I don't know that he will survive being near a pack of wolves."

Alessandra stared at me for a moment before rummaging in her pocketbook. She pulled out a little vial and set it on the table. "Let's see if it dulls the stench any."

John finished his sandwich, wiped his hands and mouth with a napkin, and then picked up the vial.

"It's undiluted, so hopefully you don't have a reaction."

"I usually use a carrier oil, but I have put this directly on achy joints." He poured at least ten drops on his hands, rubbed them together and then wiped his hands on his arms, neck and head, but stayed away from his face.

Peppermint penetrated the air, dulling his vile smell to the point it wasn't triggering the attack response.

Robert even seemed to relax.

Alessandra nodded and glanced at me. "I can work with this. Plus, it gives us an easier alibi with Archer. We can tell him John is sick and the undertones he's smelling are the disease. John combats some of the more painful symptoms with peppermint oil. And he's only staying with us until his surgery is approved and scheduled. Plus, we can tell Archer that the more contact we have with John, the more his condition flares up."

Okay. My wife can spin one hell of a tall tale—it was believable and ensured that John would stay in the apartment until he got the call.

CHAPTER 15

ALESSANDRA BOUGHT A METRIC fuckton of peppermint essential oil on our way home so John would have it on hand. She also bought some extra-virgin olive oil in the event he had any reaction from using the oil directly on his skin. And she was the one to get him settled into the apartment.

I rolled into the house to Archer pacing the living room floor, biting a hangnail.

"What's up?"

He lifted a shoulder and glanced toward the hall where their bedroom and nursery were set up. "She's talking on the phone with her parents."

Surprise raked over my skin. Her parents hadn't reached out at all, even over the holidays. "Really?"

He nodded. "She wanted to see if they wanted to come to graduation." He cocked his head. "Why do you smell like peppermint? And where's Mom?"

Leveraging Alessandra's story, I answered, "She's getting a sick guest settled. He needed a place to wait for surgery. He uses peppermint to help with the pains of his disease." Archer's eyes widened, and I knew exactly where his mind went. "And no, it's not anything transmittable, so you and Cheryl are safe. But interactions with him makes his pain worse, so we shouldn't be visiting if we can help it."

"Oh. Okay." He went back to chewing his nails.

Cheryl came out of the bedroom, her face scrunched in annoyance. Her belly protruded enough to announce her late stage of pregnancy to anyone looking at her. Her face was a rash of red, and her dark hair looked as if she was pulling at it in aggravation.

Archer's eyebrows rose.

"My parents are assholes. Remind me of that if they decide they want to be a part of our child's life."

Archer went to her and gave her a hug. "Don't worry. I won't let them anywhere near our kids."

His fierce response brought a smile to my face. "I'm sorry your parents haven't come around." I couldn't imagine cutting my child off. Being disappointed, oh yeah. But walking away? Nope. Not me, and certainly not Alessandra. After seven months under my roof, I even considered Cheryl my daughter and not just through marriage.

"At least I have you and Leigh," she said, using my nickname for Alessandra.

"Always." I headed toward my spot across from the television. I needed something to take my mind off the fact we had a witch who practiced dark magic on the premises.

GRADUATION CAME AND WENT, and Cheryl's parents ignored her accomplishment. And John was still with us, layering peppermint on himself to avoid being attacked. The kids had a handful of interactions with him over the last month and a half, but thankfully nothing raised flags.

John's new identification was due within the next couple of days, and I was just as antsy to have him gone as Alessandra. The one benefit he provided during his stay was he painted runes on the apartment walls, so whatever magic he practiced inside those walls was suppressed. The agency couldn't detect a thing. I asked him to do that with the house, too. Having that kind of protection was essential for any of the supernaturals staying with us. We now had less of a chance of being detected. Even so, any time the doorbell rang, I stiffened, thinking that perhaps the agency had sniffed us out.

The file on my desk irked me as I browsed the list of infractions. It was bad enough that the complaints came from our pack, but the kicker of the issue was it involved Cheryl's parents.

The knock on my doorframe lifted my gaze. Alessandra leaned against the wood. She had been the one to give me the file and had been patient with me while I read through the many situations.

I leaned back in my seat. "I don't know what to do with this."

"Do I have the authority to exile them from the pack?"

I blew air out between my lips. They were using silver to keep their nephew in line. They apparently didn't want a repeat of what happened with Cheryl in the family, and their nephew was orphaned earlier this year. They had threatened neighbors and anyone else who found out what they were doing, and even threatened bodily harm to those who they suspected might know of their actions if word got to Alessandra.

All of it was unacceptable. I guess they must have forgotten that Alessandra had the pulse of the pack at her disposal. She felt the unsettled air and reached out to those who were emitting downright frightened vibes. She usually could tell the difference between family squabbles and an authentic problem. And this was a mother of a problem.

Based on the laws the council had passed, their transgression of using silver to control their nephew was a capital crime. As alpha, Alessandra had the right to tear them apart. And as the head of the council, I had the right to bury a bullet in their brains.

"They are committing a capital offense." I couldn't go easy on them because they were Cheryl's parents.

Alessandra's jaw dropped. "But…"

"But what? I cannot let personal connections impact my judgment. I need to bring this to the council."

She crossed her arms. "It's a situation within our pack."

"You brought it to the council." I waved at the folder on my desk.

She closed the door behind her. "I brought it to my husband." She crossed and leaned on the desk, glaring at me.

I pointed at her. "Don't even..."

"You will not bring this to the council." Her alpha command rolled over me, and I gritted my teeth. I had the power to ignore her order. I had done it a thousand times over the years, when I knew she was wrong, but it still goaded me to no end.

I slammed my palm on the desk. "Fucking hell, Leigh. I cannot be compromised like this. It puts my integrity on the line."

"And offering it up to the council undermines my alpha authority."

She wasn't budging on this, and I could see her point. But it still didn't help the slew of questions I'd have to answer for not bringing this immediately to the other council members.

"What about their nephew?" I tossed out. Because if she exiled them, they might insist on bringing him along and continue to torture the poor kid.

She straightened. "I'll give him the option of staying if he chooses." She closed her eyes and sighed. "I'll call a meeting of the elders and will have Hans and Nathan bring them in with their nephew. I will do it here so you, Archer, and Cheryl can witness the outcome."

I nodded curtly, still very unhappy with my wife's choice to attempt to use her alpha commands on me.

CHAPTER 16

I WAS THE LAST one to enter our great room. Alessandra had the furniture pushed against the walls and the elders sitting around the outer space of the room. In the center, Hans and Nathan stood behind George and Tabitha. Their low growls seemed to keep the Carsons from bolting.

Archer and Cheryl were behind Alessandra, sitting on the couch together, looking just as confused as most of the faces in the room.

I rolled up next to them, waiting for all hell to break loose.

Alessandra held the file in her hand and opened it while silence descended. Her fury blanketed the room, nearly drawing everyone into a hunch from the weight of it.

"Why are we here?" George ground out the words between his clenched teeth.

The front door opened and a group of George's neighbors, followed by John, shuffled into the space. Peppermint swept through the room, mixing with Alessandra's fury. I hadn't expected John to be present. Nor did I expect he'd have a basket with vials filled with clear liquid.

Alessandra gave him a nod, and he handed the vials to the people who entered with him, leaving only three left in the basket.

"This is a friend of ours who is staying until he gets called in for surgery. He has experience with truth serums." She nodded at the vials in the pack member's hands.

John crossed and handed her the last three before retreating to a chair near where I sat.

Alessandra stared George down. "Will you drink this willingly?"

"You bitch." George lunged forward, but Nathan grabbed his arms, holding him in place. Hans still held one of Tabitha's arms, but she didn't seem to be a flight risk or an outright danger the way George seemed to be.

"I guess that's a no." She looked at their nephew. "Kane, will you?"

He hunched over as if in constant pain. His face was pinched as he looked at his aunt and uncle with trepidation. But he nodded. His light hair lay limp on his pimpled forehead. The young teenager shuffled forward.

"Don't—"

"Shut it." Alessandra's command shut down George.

"What's going on?" Cheryl whispered to Archer as Kane downed the liquid, along with the others who had come in with John.

"No idea." Archer glanced at me.

I just shook my head. They'd hear the damning evidence soon enough.

Alessandra kept her gaze on George. "Kane, can you tell us what has been going on at your uncle's home?"

He grimaced. "After my parents died in that car crash, they took me in. And I was happy at first, but the minute I took an interest in a girl down the road, he got unreasonably irate." He seemed to pick his words so he could be within the truth parameters of the serum. And he kept his gaze on the ground.

"Define unreasonably irate." Alessandra stepped closer and tilted his chin up so he could see her. "There will be no retribution for telling us the truth."

His chin quivered, and his gaze fluttered from Alessandra to Cheryl and then back. "They didn't want me to be like his disowned daughter, and they made sure that wouldn't happen."

So far, there was no evidence as to the notes in the file. Only that a parental figure was stricter than most. But there was so much more to this than he had been drilled into saying. The story he told was spun well, but we all could smell the swell of fear in the room.

"How did he make sure, Kane?"

"Silver," Kane hissed and cowered at the growl from his uncle.

"He threatened you with silver?" Cheryl asked, now on her feet. Her anger nearly matched Alessandra's.

A tear dropped from Kane's eye. "Not threatened." His answer was just a whisper.

"Show me." The command from Alessandra rang through the room.

Kane's face turned beet red, but he couldn't refuse his alpha's command.

When Kane reached for his belt, my stomach clenched. The file had just said they used silver to keep him in line. The kid's eyes pleaded for the order to stop, but Alessandra just looked on without flinching, until the boy dropped his pants.

A gasp went through the room at the silver cock ring around the base of the teenager's member. The blackened skin visible around the silver had me nearly drawing my gun and killing George.

"What the fuck?" Cheryl blurted, and her gaze jumped to her father.

Alessandra put her hand out, silencing Cheryl and anyone else from speaking. She turned to the only non-werewolf in the room. "Can you remove that?"

John waved his hand and the silver ring split in two, falling to the ground at the boy's feet. His nonchalant manner impressed me, but the magic that fell over the room had my nostrils flaring.

All eyes turned in his direction.

"He's harmless," Alessandra said, pushing the command out and bringing eyes back to her.

"Do you have a healing salve or elixir?" she asked John.

His lips twitched, and he pulled out a small vial from his pocket, handing it to her. She held it out to Kane, and he took it without question.

"That should help you heal faster." She waited until he pulled his pants back into place before turning her icy stare at George and Tabitha. "Do you have anything to say? Or should I continue with the testimony of your neighbors and acquaintances who you threatened?"

"We didn't want another disgrace."

"And you believe you had the right to do what you did?"

"We are his guardians. We have the right to oversee his life as we see fit."

"Bullshit." Cheryl was on her feet. "You used silver. That leaves a permanent burn." Her belly protruded before her, and the way she stood showed just how close to term her pregnancy was. "You have no right to be a parent when you so easily discarded your only daughter. And then you abuse your guardianship of Kane in this manner? You are the disgrace."

"You do realize using silver to torture a werewolf is a capital offense, right?" Archer stepped next to Cheryl and put his hand on her lower back in a show of support.

"Pft. It wasn't torture, it was prevention."

"I beg to differ." Kane glared at his guardian and uncorked the vial, downing it as if his action were more of a rebellion. Then he crossed to Cheryl and slung his arm over her shoulders. "And she is not a disgrace."

Archer traded a nod of acknowledgment with Kane.

George and Tabitha let out growls as their faces turned almost beet red with anger. If the elders hadn't been present, they surely would have turned into their wolves and attacked.

Alessandra glanced at me before she looked at the rest of the elders. "I am seeking your verdict, since I have a personal connection with the accused beyond being the alpha of the pack."

They nodded and Samuel, the eldest of the elders, asked, "May we step away for a moment?"

"Yes." Alessandra nodded toward the door to my study. "You can use Hunter's study."

My soundproof office was a necessity. Cases discussed between council members were not fit for public consumption, especially sensitive ones that required confidentiality. And the pack was aware of the arrangements and accommodations made in this house, since some of them helped with the modifications.

The moment the elders left, the tension in the room increased. One glare from George had the witnesses quaking. Even the muscle of Hans and Nathan keeping them in place couldn't wipe their fear away from those the Carsons threatened.

And Cheryl's anger seemed to add to the unease. Especially with her parents now aiming their gaze her way. They stared at her as if she were a diseased bug.

Everything about this was unacceptable, and all I wanted to do was empty my revolver in their hides. Their lack of compassion for their own child astounded me, and now this heinous treatment of their charge just added to my anger. I hated to think what they would do to my grandchild if given the chance.

My back tensed against a shiver. I couldn't allow them to continue glaring that way at my daughter-in-law.

I rolled in front of Cheryl, giving them another target to glower at. Despite being confined to a wheelchair, I could make my presence and my disdain just as loud as Alessandra's. After all, I was the beta of this pack.

Alessandra put her hand on my shoulder as if reading my volatile emotions accurately. I wanted control of the meeting, and I craved justice being served. And these two needed to be taken down. But I wasn't in charge right now.

The door to my office opened after what seemed much longer than I thought it would take, and the pack elders filed back into the room, all with stern expressions on their faces. As soon as they gathered outside my office, Samuel gave Alessandra a nod.

"While the council's law states that this infraction is a capital offense, we will leave the punishment to you, Alpha."

I glanced at Alessandra as she nodded at Samuel and the elders. With a deep breath, she moved her gaze to George and Tabitha.

"As Samuel pointed out, this type of abuse is a capital offense. And while I'd like nothing more than to tear you to pieces for what you have done, I will show mercy because you are related to my daughter-in-law."

George's face broke out in a smug smile.

"So, I give you your life, but I exile you from the pack. I will give you an hour to get off pack lands. If you ever set foot within our boundaries, you will be executed."

The air in the room buzzed as Alessandra severed George and Tabitha from the pack bond.

It took George a moment to realize what Alessandra said, and then his growl became feral. He broke away from Nathan and lunged forward with a knife in his hand. The blade whistled close to Alessandra, but she ducked out of the way.

I rolled forward, intercepting him before he could recover from missing her. I grabbed his hand and pulled to the side while I drew my gun and squeezed the trigger. The bullet exploded out his back and wedged into the ceiling. George fell over my lap.

Tabitha gripped her hair and screamed as I shoved George's dead body off me.

I pointed the gun at her. "You did nothing to stop this."

"I-I," she stuttered, unable to deny my accusation. "I didn't know," she finally whispered.

Kane scoffed from behind me. "This was your idea, not his."

Her frightened gaze turned sharp as it jumped to Kane.

"Um, Hunter?" Alessandra said.

"What?" I didn't take my gaze off Tabitha.

"You need a doctor."

I didn't dare look at whatever Alessandra was looking at. Instead, I said to Tabitha, "Exile or death?"

The smile that twerked her lips as she looked at my lap nearly made me look down, but she didn't utter a word beyond the satisfied grin that appeared.

Her choice was made for her when a wolf launched past me and ripped her throat to shreds in seconds.

That wolf was not Alessandra. She was at my side with John. My brain went fuzzy as the wolf shifted and the image of Archer standing next to Tabitha's dead body with blood smeared on his face came into focus.

"Get everyone out and I'll fix him," John whispered.

The wolves in the room were too stunned at the quick turnaround. Plus, their ears were still ringing from the gunshot, so thankfully, John's statement was lost on them.

"Everybody but my family out!" Alessandra commanded.

The room cleared quickly, although the smell of blood and feces nearly made me gag. When John lifted me out of the chair and laid me on the floor, I still wasn't aware of my damage.

"What are you doing?" Archer nearly threw John off me.

"He's a powerful witch. Let him help." Alessandra glanced at Cheryl and then back at Archer. "You might need to tend to your wife."

He glanced at her, then at Cheryl, and stepped away.

John chanted under his breath with his hands over my abdomen. Heat enveloped me. I lifted my head enough to look, and I immediately wished I hadn't. George had ripped through my abdomen and left the damn knife embedded in my flesh. Flesh blackened by silver. The asshole had used a fucking silver knife.

I dropped my head back on the carpet.

Alessandra took my hand and squeezed as she kneeled at my side, watching John do his thing. She winced when John pulled the blade out. But he was still chanting and light cascaded from his hands.

Instead of watching his magic, I stared at the awe filling Alessandra's face. Her eyes widened and her lips opened in a way that had me wanting to kiss her instead of coping with being on death's door.

"It's no wonder Robert wanted to hide you." The words were out before she could stop them, and her gaze slashed to mine. Her eyes widened, and she turned to Archer and Cheryl.

Archer stared at us with Cheryl in his arms, but the puzzlement line between his eyes announced he had heard his mother. But at least he had the sense to not make a big deal of it. His hands were full with Cheryl as the reality that both her parents were dead left her a sobbing mess.

John reached into his pocket and handed Alessandra a vial that looked like the one Kane had taken. "Make him drink." And then he began chanting again.

Alessandra dumped the contents down my throat without hesitation.

I only had a fleeting taste of citrus before it hit my stomach. A bomb of heat spread through me, making my toes actually tingle. I hadn't had that type of reaction since the night Archer had been conceived. I blinked and tried to wiggle my toes, but nothing happened.

When John finished chanting, I asked, "You don't have any more of that elixir left, do you?"

"Sorry. No. I had made two batches as a failsafe." He wiped his forehead and glanced at the state of our living room. "Why?"

"Because I thought my toes tingled."

Silence fell over the room. Even Cheryl's whimpering stopped.

"You what?" Alessandra asked.

Before I could speak, John raised his hand to stop her. "A tingling sensation is normal when the magic works. While I can mend cuts and suck out silver poisoning from the blood, I cannot heal a broken spine. If I had that kind of angelic magic, I would have fixed you on my first week here."

I closed my eyes and turned my head. When I opened them, my gaze landed on the dead littering our living room, along with all the bits and pieces splattered on the ceiling and walls.

"We are going to need this professionally cleaned." I wiped my face and sighed.

"Why are you here?" Archer asked, pulling all our attention to him.

"Your mother asked me if I could make some truth serum and a healing elixir for her, and if I knew how to reverse the effects of silver poisoning."

"No. I mean living over our garage?"

"I'm waiting for an operation." He used the agreed-upon story.

Archer shook his head. "Then why would you need to be hidden?"

John chewed on his bottom lip and traded a glance with me. "Well, you've smelled the disease, right?" He twirled his finger. "Even with the peppermint, it can leak out and it apparently causes wolves to get hostile."

He was good. That was just enough of the truth to settle Archer.

"If I don't get in for surgery soon, even the peppermint won't help and then I'm as good as dead. So, considering I'm a witch who has been around supernaturals all my life, this affliction makes it so I need to be in a safe place until the call comes in." He glanced at me and then Alessandra. "Your parents have a reputation in the community, and I reached out for help."

"Oh." Archer seemed satisfied with the answer, and it looked like the stress of this situation was behind us.

And then Cheryl cried out as a river of water gushed from between her legs.

CHAPTER 17

"DID YOU JUST PEE on the floor?" Archer asked.

Alessandra burst out laughing.

I just stared at the mess from my prone position and laid my head back down. "You should take her to the hospital."

Archer's face blanched. "Why?"

Cheryl cried out and doubled over.

John muttered under his breath, and magic filled the air. His eyes widened. "No time for that." He dumped me back into my chair, leaving me to my own devices. "She needs to be in a clean environment, though."

Alessandra grabbed his arm as he headed toward Archer and Cheryl.

"I've delivered dozens of babies. It will be fine. Just help your husband clean himself up and then meet us in their bedroom." He turned back to the kids.

Archer's eyes were much wider than they had been. "Labor?"

"It's too early," Cheryl said, through another gasp.

"Well, he's coming out within the half hour." John glanced at Archer. "You need to clean off quickly, but before you do, bring me towels."

He escorted Archer and Cheryl back to their room, and Alessandra pushed me to our shower.

"Clean up and I'll get your chair done."

I moved myself to my shower chair and stripped as fast as I could, which for a paraplegic isn't quick, especially with pants from a sitting position. I ended up just shredding the material to get it off and turned on the water, scrubbing the blood from my abdomen and legs until the water ran clear. I had not realized just how much blood I had lost. It gave me a new appreciation for John and the level of magic he held.

Alessandra wheeled my clean chair to me and handed me the towel hanging over the bar. It wasn't quite dry, but I didn't care.

She helped me pull on underwear and my sweatpants and then towel dried my hair before rolling me shirtless to the other side of the house in nearly a sprint. It took me less than twenty minutes to clean up. Which was a new record for me, and I only got there because Alessandra helped. She was motivated and just as eager to see our grandchild enter the world as I was.

We rolled into the room just as Cheryl pushed out a head. The next push, the entire body shot into a towel that John held.

John picked up a plastic chip-clip from the fold-up table Archer must have gotten while we were cleaning up. A pair of scissors, a bowl of clean water, and a clean washcloth sat on the table as well. John clamped the cord with the clip and then handed Archer the sharp shears. "You do the honors." He held a piece of the umbilical cord out for Archer to cut.

Archer stilled the shakes in his hand and cut through the cord.

John dipped the washcloth into the clean water and cleaned the baby before swaddling it in another clean towel. He laid the child on Cheryl's chest. "You have a beautiful baby boy."

The placenta came next and then it was over, and John piled all the soiled towels on the ground and sighed. "Next time you do this, make sure you have a midwife on the premises when you are within a month of delivery. You won't make it to the hospital then, either."

I just sat in the doorway and stared at that little boy on my daughter-in-law's chest. If they had attempted to drive to the hospital, that child would have been born in the car.

John stepped over to the desk and scribbled on a piece of paper the date and time. He also wrote the weight and length of the baby as well.

I cocked an eyebrow at him.

"I used magic to get the measurements and weight." He smirked at me and glanced at the kids. "What's his name?"

"Kyle Jacob Blaez." Cheryl smiled.

My heart just about exploded with pride in my chest.

John wrote that on the paper as well. "You'll need this for a birth certificate." He handed the paper to Archer. "Whenever you decide to head to the hospital to have them checked out."

"How can we repay you for this?" Alessandra asked.

"No need. This is my pleasure. There is nothing more gratifying than delivering a baby." He looked around the room. "And this is my gift to you for all you have done for me." He looked at her and then waved his hands. Magic swelled in the room. The blood and other liquids soaked into the towels and bed trailed off, leaving only pristinely clean fabric. He turned and walked with the mess rolling in front of him like a living thing.

I watched from the door as he did the same with the living room, rolling all the blood and gore into a single mound of grossness that he pushed into the fireplace, along with the bodies of George and Tabitha. With another wave of his hand, they ignited. Burning fast and furious until nothing was left in the fireplace but ash and soot.

That was a damn powerful witch, and I was glad he was on our side.

"I'm going to go get some rest." He gave me a nod and left the house just as pristine as when he had walked in the door.

I turned my focus back to the bedroom. "Well, we don't need cleaners anymore." I rolled to the side of the bed and smiled at the baby.

"Do you want to hold him?" Archer asked.

I glanced at Alessandra. She wanted to get her hands on the child, too. "Let your mother have first dibs on holding our grandchild." I could wait. Besides, I was still recovering some from my near-death experience.

CHAPTER 18

"WHAT IS THIS?" CHERYL asked as she un-swaddled Kyle to put him in a diaper before he soiled her or the nice clean bed John had left behind.

Alessandra and Archer looked over her shoulder. Their mouths dropped open for a fraction of a second. Archer's clamped shut and a line of irritation wedged itself between his eyes. Alessandra glanced back at me with a smile.

"It looks like Kyle is the next alpha of our pack," she said.

Archer's reaction made much more sense. Until this moment, he believed he might still be given the mark. What he failed to understand was that he never had the alpha authority.

As for my new grandson, I could feel the authority radiating from Kyle. It was much the same with Alessandra as a child. As a wolf in the pack, you wanted to follow her and protect her. That was the same instinct that flared in me when I rolled forward and saw the mark on the baby on the changing table.

"He's so young." I glanced up at her. After all, her mark didn't come until she was in college.

"My dad had the mark at birth." She beamed.

I nodded. I remembered our prior alpha. He had given his daughter a litany of warnings she had never heeded. I always wondered whether that was why the mark hadn't shown up earlier.

I glanced up at Archer and Cheryl. They both wore the same look: fierce pride and a bit of melancholy. They would never be at the head of the pack.

THE PAPERS FOR JOHN came a couple of days later. I sent Alessandra over to retrieve him.

"Hey." John walked into the office and closed the door behind him. "How are you feeling?"

"I'm good. After all the excitement, I got enough sleep to be back to my old self again."

He grinned. "Plus, I imagine having a little one sleeping on your shoulder is a source of peace and tranquility." He nodded toward Kyle curled up on my shoulder.

I rubbed his little back and nodded. "I was terrified to be a father when Archer came, but with this one, I have zero tension. I love being a grandfather."

John's smile soured, and he gave me a noncommittal nod. Unless he found someone and had another kid, he'd never know this pure joy.

I picked up the envelope in front of me and held it out to him. "You are all set. Your flight leaves tonight."

He took a seat in the chair and looked through the documents I handed him. Once he examined everything, he said, "This is impressive."

"No. What you did the other day was impressive. This is just creating a fictitious person and their life circumstances on paper tight enough to dupe everyone. It isn't magic." My lip twitched at the edges.

"Never sell yourself short like that. What you are doing here is saving lives, but in a different way. This is impressive as hell to me, and I've been out there, looking at fake documentation for years. I would pass this as real." He fanned the envelope. "Robert said you were a rare soul. I agree. Thank you for giving me a new lease on life."

I hated this part. I always felt humbled by the acknowledgment of my part in this routine. Especially because I didn't feel like a savior of souls.

"I'll get you to the airport."

"It's okay. I can get there on my own."

I appreciated that, but it still left me on edge. I wanted to be sure he got out of this country with his life intact. If he died on our soil, I would have failed in my job to keep him safe. "If it's all the same to you, I'd still like to take you for my peace of mind. Especially after you saved my life."

He glanced at the package in his hand. "No. You enjoy your grandson. I assure you, I am no longer in danger. Besides, if the agency is still scanning for facial recognition, I don't want you to be tagged as the one to drop me at the airport. That would bring on an entirely different scrutiny that your family cannot afford." His eyes lowered to my grandson.

"Point taken," I conceded. "Just text me a note when you are settled, then."

"That I can do." He stood and extended his hand. "It has been a pleasure." His handshake was firm, and then he dropped my hand and headed toward the door. "Tell your son not to forget what I said about timing if they ever decide on a second child." And then he was gone.

I never saw John again. But a few days later, I got a random text with a picture of a beach and the turquoise water beyond.

CHAPTER 19

TIME SLIPPED AWAY FROM us all. Before we knew it, Kyle was getting ready for nursery school, the house we built for Archer and Cheryl on the acre next to ours was almost ready to move into, and Cheryl was pregnant again.

I was certainly going to miss the constant chaos once they moved out, but Alessandra and I craved the quiet we had when Archer was in high school. We needed a little alone time, especially considering I had been experiencing more health issues related to my condition. Alessandra had pack responsibilities, and I still had the council. Plus, we'd had a few more of Robert's refugees come through. At least the last couple had been witches or wolves, and none of them had a stench like John.

And we all remembered John's warning about Cheryl and her pregnancies. So once the word was out, we hired Lina, the pack midwife, to take care of Cheryl. As soon as Cheryl hit eight and a half months, Lina moved into the garage apartment so she could be close by in the event of a repeat.

That turned out to be a blessing because once Cheryl hit the ninth month, she started having contractions. This time, she knew what they were and gave Archer a heads-up.

I don't think I've ever seen him sprint across the driveway at that pace in human form before. If we weren't so on edge about another delivery, I would have laughed. But we were busy prepping the bedroom, so it was a quick cleanup rather than a scrub fest. A large plastic tarp was laid out over the bed and stretched out on the floor. A clean fitted sheet we were planning on getting rid of covered the plastic, so Cheryl had something more comfortable against her skin.

Basins of water and older towels were also spread about the room. A table with a clean blanket to swaddle the little one was also set out. When Cheryl walked back in the room with a handful of towels, she glanced at the setup and raised an eyebrow.

"John's not around to magically clean this place up," I answered as Alessandra left the room to go grab the rest of the items on the list that Lina had given her.

Her smile faded. "Do you know if he survived the surgery?"

I thought back to that text I received and nodded. He survived the trip and now had a new identity. I didn't know whether he stayed in Haiti or not, but I imagined he'd have a nice quiet beach cabana and was enjoying the hell out of life.

Cheryl hissed through her teeth and nearly doubled over.

I blinked away a flashback of the last time this happened. Water gushed down her legs, but this time, she was on the tarp. I threw a towel down to soak up the fluid before it reached the wood floor, and my heart jumpstarted into overdrive because I was the only one in the room with her.

"Why don't you get comfortable? I'm going to see what's taking Archer." I rolled backward toward the door.

"Don't go," she said.

"Okay." I rolled to the side of the bed and waited for her to get situated.

Alessandra stepped into the room, looking more harried than usual. She tried to smile, but it was forced. "Um. Hunter. You have a guest in your office."

I stared at her as if she had grown another head. "Where's Archer and Lina?"

"They're coming. But you need to go." She pointed toward my office, and I rolled away, but she had already switched into nurse mode with Cheryl.

I rolled down the hall just as Archer and Lina jogged by. Neither one of them acknowledged me; they just slid by my wheelchair like I wasn't even there. I couldn't blame them. Cheryl's last delivery was in the forefront of all our minds.

All thoughts of the new baby blew out of my mind as I opened my office door. Robert Young paced in front of my desk. His hand ran through his hair, spiking it. His eyes were so bloodshot that even the blue of his irises looked like blood vessels had popped. I had never seen him so disheveled. Even the time he was attacked, he was in total control of his emotions.

"What happened?" I closed the door behind me and turned my wheelchair in his direction.

He shook his head, dropped into one of the chairs in front of my desk, and covered his face with his hand. "I got him killed."

His muttered response sent a cold chill through me. "Who?" I rolled closer.

"My son." Pain laced those words.

I couldn't fathom that kind of loss. And Robert had had more than his share of devastating cards dealt to him already. I rolled to his side and placed my hand on his shoulder, offering what little I could.

"I didn't get to tell him I was proud of him." Robert lifted his tear-stained face and stared at me as if I could bring the kid back from the dead.

I squeezed his shoulder and then rolled back, giving him some room. "Would you like to tell me about it?"

At first, he just shook his head until he had a little more control. Then he took a deep breath and launched into it. "Another fucking vampire." He wiped his face. "You want to know the kicker?"

I nodded.

"His fated mate, you know, the one I was supposed to keep him from? Well, that bitch killed him." A dry, humorless laugh rasped out of his mouth. "Her new master told me he died by her hand."

"Fuck." The word slipped out before I could stop it. Robby had been at the council meetings religiously since he took over as alpha. I actually respected Robert's son. That alpha was one of the best I had met outside of Alessandra. His pack came first, and although there were a few disagreements as to how to handle some items over the years, he treated me with respect.

If he hadn't worked for the agency, he would have been offered a spot on the council a few years back when we lost one of the aging members. And the alphas would have unanimously voted him onto the board. Not only was that a loss to his pack, it was a loss to the council.

His gaze hardened. "Yup. If I ever get my hands on that bitch, I am going to kill her slowly."

I had no doubt about that. Murderous vibes flowed off Robert. Enough to make me want to get away from him before he decided to exact that wrath on the closest person.

After a few deep breaths, he reined in his fury and gave me an apologetic smile. "Sorry."

"You have nothing to apologize to me for."

He didn't reply. Instead, he slipped a piece of paper from his pocket and handed it to me. "I need this person to be accepted by the council as the new alpha. He was Robby's beta and an extremely loyal soul. He loved my son like a brother and did his damnedest to keep Robby safe."

I glanced at the name and nodded. I had met Robby's beta a few times at the annual meetings. "Done." I took a breath. "What else do you need?"

His lip quirked up on one side. "I might need your services if my plans to take down this fucking agency go awry."

"I'll be here if you need me."

Robert looked at the ceiling and wiped the grief off his face, replacing it with a steel resolve that worried me.

Before I could ask him what he was planning, power sizzled through the house. Both our gazes darted to the door. I rolled toward it, unsure of what I might find on the other side. The minute the door opened, another blast of alpha power rang through the house, followed by the wail of a newborn baby.

I let out a surprised laugh. It looked like Cheryl delivered another alpha, and this one was strong. He couldn't possibly have a mark, could he?

"Damn. New grandchild?" Robert asked as he stood.

"Sounds like it." Kyle hadn't gotten home from school yet, so that cry could only be from their newborn.

"That alpha signature is as strong as Robby's was when he was born," Robert said in a voice rough with emotion. He passed by me and headed toward the front door. "I'll be in touch."

He slipped out before I could process his comment. Robby was an exceptionally powerful alpha. If the new baby was that strong, they would need their own pack someday. He or she wouldn't be able to stay and be subservient to another wolf, even if that wolf was their brother.

CHAPTER 20

I ROLLED INTO THE bedroom as Lina was cleaning the baby. In my brief visit with Robert, the baby and placenta were delivered, and Alessandra and Archer were in the midst of cleaning the localized mess up and depositing it into a bucket bound for the garbage.

Cheryl stepped out of the bathroom with a fresh set of clothing, looking tired, but not as exhausted as she had been after Kyle's birth. But then again, this delivery took half the time and there wasn't the emotional punch of losing her parents moments before labor started.

"Another boy," Archer announced with a grin. "Logan." He looked at the bassinet. "It seems he's got quite a demanding presence, too."

Alessandra met my gaze, and she gave me the kind of look that silenced me. She had to have felt this little guy's power, but for some reason, she didn't want me saying anything about it.

"Is that so?" I rolled to where Lina was just finishing up and looked down into the bright-blue eyes of the newborn. "Hi there, Logan."

His gaze darted to me, and a flare of protectiveness sped through my form. He was even cuter than Kyle had been and so much more attentive. I'd have to be the one to educate this one on how an alpha should act because I had a feeling he was destined for something more than just being a shadow.

Alessandra would be busy grooming Kyle, and neither Archer nor Cheryl knew the first thing about being an alpha, so the responsibility fell on my shoulders to teach him the proper way to be an alpha. And that had nothing to do with being a bully and everything with being a leader.

Cheryl crawled into the clean bed and put her arms out for the baby. Lina promptly deposited the newborn in her arms.

"I'll go get this filed for you." Lina waved the birth certificate and then grabbed the bucket of garbage and left the room.

As soon as Logan was nestled into Cheryl's arms, Alessandra crossed and stepped behind me. "I'll give you two some quiet time with Logan before Kyle gets home from school."

I would have liked a little more time with my grandson, but I didn't argue with my wife as she pushed me back to my office and closed the door.

"Did you feel it?" she asked quietly.

"Yes. Both Robert and I felt the blast of his power." I turned toward her.

"I don't know what Archer and Cheryl felt, but as the alpha of this pack, I recognized a threat to my station within my territory." She exhaled. "It was so much stronger than Kyle's alpha presence. But no mark. I'm not sure how that's going to go within our pack."

I nodded. "Are you sure that feeling wasn't because Robert was here?" He was an alpha, after all.

"Yes. I was uneasy with him in the house, but it wasn't the same."

"Logan will be fine," I said, but wasn't as sure as I sounded. Especially if Kyle viewed him as a threat. Alphas were territorial to a fault. It amazed me that Alessandra never got antsy with all the alphas in town for the annual meeting. I'm not sure I would be as calm and commanding as she was, but then again, I didn't have the mark, either.

"What did Robert want, anyway?"

"His son died, and he gave me the name of the next alpha and asked me to clear it with the council."

Pain flashed through our bond. "Oh, no. He was such a role model for the other alphas." Her eyes filled with tears, but she blinked them back. "Is Robert taking over again?"

"No. It's Robby's beta. Rick Johnson. We've met him during at least one council meeting. I told him it's cleared."

"Jake." She sighed.

"I know. It's a requirement to vote on it, but considering the circumstances and the fact that their pack is still under the agency and not the council, I think I have the latitude to make this call."

She gave me that disappointed look.

"I will talk to the council. I doubt there will be any dissention. Besides, there's no one for Johnson to challenge for the position."

Alessandra shuddered. A challenge meant a fight to the death and the victor would take the alpha position in the pack. There had been a few of those over the years, but usually a death sentence was something that deterred challenges.

We stared at each other.

Someday, Logan would throw a challenge out. I just prayed it wasn't for the alpha position in our pack.

CHAPTER 21

WE STARED AT THE news on television in shock. I reached out for Alessandra's hand, and she squeezed as we scanned the destruction. The Monster Defense Agency building in New York City was literally ashes. Robert flashed in my mind and then, in the corner of the screen, I saw him arrive on scene.

My heart thundered as he appeared to be arguing with someone behind the reporter.

I glanced at Alessandra. She had seen the same thing, and we both exhaled in relief. He hadn't perished in that building.

"You think this was him?" she asked quietly, trying not to wake Logan, who slept on the couch by her. I knew exactly who she was referring to. We hadn't seen him since the day Logan was born.

"I'd bet money on it. Especially after the slaughter of the vampires a few days ago. But damned if I know how the hell he pulled it all off."

My phone started to buzz, and I scanned the messages from the other council members. They wanted me to call an emergency meeting right now. I texted back asking that we wait until more information came out before we panicked. I really wanted time to hear from Robert and get an update from the source before we held a meeting, but I couldn't say that. Instead, I agreed to meet a week from today.

I sent out the request for a mandatory council meeting to all the alphas and included Robert's personal email as a blind copy. It came back as undeliverable. I would just have to wait until all the alphas and the agency representatives arrived at the meeting to find out what the hell was going on.

AS THE ALPHAS FILTERED into the town hall for the mandatory meeting, Alessandra and I kept our game faces on. My chest constricted each time the door opened. The room was nearly full when Rick Johnson stepped in, followed by a face that stole the breath from my chest.

Robert's son followed the Allegany pack alpha into the room, and a hush fell over the space.

Robby Young had the look of a prisoner of war. He was thinner than the last time he graced us with his presence, but it was his haunted gaze that made me swallow hard. His eyes darted around until they landed on me.

I looked beyond him, expecting his father to step in behind him, but the door shut. The click sent my stomach tumbling, and I cleared my throat, glancing at the other members of the council. I received nods to open the meeting.

"It seems all the alphas are present." I glanced directly at Robby Young as I spoke wondering whether he might have the answers we sought. "The reason we called you all here is because of the destruction in New York City. With the recent extinction of vampires, I know there is a worry that our species will be targeted next. But before we jump to any conclusions, I'd like to open the floor to any reports on the chaos we saw reported from the city."

Rick Johnson stepped forward and nodded for Robby to join him. The former alpha stepped close, but not in an equal line. It was an obvious display of respect for his alpha.

"The agency is no more," Rick said. "Robby's mate took out the head of the organization. The one pulling the strings and trapping our kind into a life of servitude."

I cocked my head as if I didn't know the ugly truth about the agency. "Servitude?" I sent a sideways glance at Alessandra. And then looked behind her at Archer. His presence at these meetings had increased since he graduated from high school. Although he'd never be an alpha, he could step in and replace me when the time came.

Robby snorted a laugh, pulling my attention back to him.

"My father said you knew about the agency," he said. "Which is why not one of you got roped into joining." He glanced around the room. "Your council head saved your lives and your packs."

"Excuse me?" Roland, the member to my right looked pointedly at me.

"Where is your father?" I asked, ignoring the accolades.

"He died at their fucking hands."

That gut twist I felt when the door clicked closed increased, and sorrow formed in the pit of my stomach. Although I had been wary of Robert over the years, he had grown on both Alessandra and me to the point I considered him a friend. I wiped my face. "There are more offices than just New York City."

"But without the head calling the shots and the vampires backing them, they don't have any muscle to push back into dominance. All the major heads were annihilated when the building came down," Rick said.

"So, your silence is no longer needed," Robby added. "These people need to know what kind of hero sits at the head of their council."

I let out a laugh. "Your father was the hero."

Robby just shook his head, but didn't expound further.

Alessandra stood. "Are you certain the danger has been eliminated?"

"Yes," both Robby and Rick said at the same time.

Alessandra looked at the other members of the council and then at the other alphas in the room. "We have always suspected the agency wasn't what it seemed. Especially with Winters running it. We knew what kind of monster Ken Winters was, and the fact he never agreed to allow the agency to poach from any of the packs associated with the council said a lot. But our suspicions were confirmed when Archer was little. Robert reached out to us to see if we would help a witch who was tagged to be killed by the agency simply because she hadn't followed through on an order."

All eyes turned to me, but it was Robby who spoke.

"The agency terminated sub-par employees. They killed anyone who questioned orders. They were monsters on a grand scale." He glanced around. "A scale sanctioned by the government. The agency had access to other monstrous beings, like vampires who they controlled. If one stepped out of line, we were called to extinguish them."

"And you just went out and killed them because you were ordered to?" Archer asked.

Robby nodded. "What do you know of vampires?"

"They are monsters that kill when they feed," Archer answered.

"So do you."

Archer blinked.

"You kill when you feed. You just don't feed on humans." He glanced around, making his point. "I agree that vampires who killed humans should be put down, just like we are if we step over that line with no valid reason. But I don't know that all the vampires we have assassinated over the years deserved it. That's a stain on my soul." He focused back on me. "But you, sir, have my utmost respect. How many people tagged for death have you saved?"

I shrugged. I didn't keep count.

"Your father was able to get dozens of people out of the agency's death sentences over the years. We housed them in our garage apartment while Hunter got them new identification." Alessandra's voice bloomed with pride.

"There were at least a hundred guests who stayed more than a couple of days over the years," Archer said.

My cheeks heated.

"And you did all that without question?" one alpha in the group asked.

"It was the right thing to do." I met his gaze.

"What if they were dangerous?" another voiced.

"What if they deserved the death sentence?" another asked.

Robby raised his hands. "No one deserves to die for who they fall in love with." Silence settled on the room. "The agency killed my family because my father broke the cardinal rule and fell in love with another one of the agents."

"Bullshit." It came from Archer.

Robby reached into his pocket and pulled out a small tape-recording device. He pressed play and a chilling conversation that happened close to thirty years ago rang out in the room. The vampire's admonishment of his father's life choices chilled my blood. When it was over, Robby clicked the recording off.

"The agency let that vampire walk. But they caged my mother for the rest of her life." Grumbles filled the room. "In a tiny cage made of silver."

"Silver cells?" Roland asked.

"Yes. They threatened us with silver all the time. Even bound us in it when restraining us. And their cages designed for werewolves had boiling silver over the cell in the event the bars were breached. I was in one of those damn things, separated from my mate, who they had across the hall."

A collective shiver went through the room. The idea of being physically separated from your mate wasn't one that any werewolf could abide.

"That's illegal," Roland said after he recovered from the shock of Robby's declarations.

"Yes. It is," I agreed with Roland.

"And were you aware of this?" His sharp gaze pierced mine.

"Not to the extent Robby just described. But I knew they employed practices we deemed illegal." I licked my lips at the rising hostility.

"If we all banded together—"

"You would have all died." Robby's interruption silenced the room. "Or did you forget the agency had witches employed and vampires to do their dirty work? They had seers as well. And they would have warned the powers that be of an attack."

"Then how did you take the agency down?" I thought his father had a hand in it. Especially because he had been charmed to not be visible to seers' predictions.

"My mate took it down."

A dozen questions popped into my head, but I kept them under wraps. I knew his mate had been his partner, which made her a witch. A powerful one, which Robert had alluded to at one point.

"So, wait, was John one of them?" Archer asked, circumventing the conversation.

I glanced at him and nodded.

"Oh." He glanced at Alessandra, and she nodded as well. He moved his open gaze to Robby, and it narrowed. "Weren't you and your partner wanted by the agency at one point?"

"Robby's mate is his partner," Rick stated.

Rumbles started throughout the room. The witch-werewolf partnerships of the agency weren't a secret.

"So, you are tainting your bloodline?" Archer crossed his arms.

I turned to him. "That's enough." I would not have any alpha speaking down to this man. From the looks of him, he had been through enough hell already, and I would not stand by and let my son ridicule him.

Alessandra glared at Archer in the same way I had. But her low growl of discontent did more to him than my snapped words. His chin fell to his chest, and he muttered an apology. But the words were out there, and the judgment was on full display in the way the other alphas viewed Robby.

"I think we are done here. We wanted to understand what happened, and Rick and Robby enlightened us." I glanced around the room and then at the council. Nods greeted me. "Go tend to your families. This matter is closed."

The alphas filtered out of the room.

"Robby, can I have a private word?" I asked before he joined the crowd.

He nodded and hung back.

"Go," I said to Alessandra and Archer.

She grabbed Archer's arm and dragged him out of the room after the last of the alphas. She closed the door to give us privacy.

I waved at the chair she had just vacated. "Have a seat."

Robby sat and studied his hands. He was a few years older than Archer, but right now, he seemed to be more of a lost boy than a man.

"Your father was proud of you."

His gaze snapped up to mine, and his eyes glossed over. He shook his head.

"When you were younger, Robert asked us to take you in if anything happened to him. He wanted you safe from harm and knew Leigh and I would protect you."

Robby leaned back in the seat as if I had slapped him. "He never mentioned you outside of council meetings."

"Your father and I had an odd friendship. He didn't have anyone he could trust, and I guess he thought I was honorable." I laughed softly.

"The guy who tore a bunch of humans to pieces because they hurt my alpha."

Robby's mouth popped open. "I thought..."

"No. That's not made up. But what the records you were privy to didn't say was they had poisoned her with belladonna, raped her, and dumped deer blood all over her, intending to kill the entire pack. One bite and we'd die with her. And Winters paid them to do it."

His face hardened in response. "Why didn't she shift and kill them before they poisoned her?"

"Our pack is unique. Besides the alpha mark situation, we also have an issue with alcohol. It prevents us from shifting, and the assholes who assaulted her knew that. They slipped alcohol in her drink at a party before abducting her."

"I would have done the same. I actually tore the vampire who turned Sarah to shreds."

That was new information, and I leaned back. "I thought when you kill the sire, it kills their offspring?"

Robby smiled. "It does, but Sarah is different in ways I do not wish to disclose."

"Robert told me she was your partner, so I know she's a witch."

Robby nodded.

"I'm sorry about your father. He wanted to make sure you knew what he sacrificed to keep you safe. You were that man's world."

Robby snorted a huff. "No, I wasn't. Revenge was his world."

"And it wasn't yours?" I cocked an eyebrow.

He pressed his lips together. "Touché." He shifted in the seat and his gaze dropped to my wheelchair and then back to my face. "Winters never thought much of you."

"Neither one of them did. Ken underestimated Leigh, and it looks as though Terrance underestimated your mate."

His smile spread slowly. "Never underestimate a woman on the warpath."

I laughed. "One of these days, I'll have to meet your warrior."

"One of these days." His smile faded. "Thank you."

"Anyone with a shred of decency would have helped."

"I wasn't referring to helping to save innocent people. I'm saying thank you for being a friend to my father. I honestly didn't think he had any genuine friends."

"I don't think he dared. He was biding his time to wage a war he wasn't sure he could win, and he didn't want to put anyone in danger. I could get a decent fake identification that passed high levels of scrutiny. So, I think it was a combination of my contacts and my discretion that he was looking for. But in the end, I think we did indeed become friends."

"And your willingness to tear anyone to pieces if they hurt your mate."

"And there's that." I nodded. I inhaled and glanced at the door. "Are you going to take back the alpha position?"

"That would require a challenge."

I nodded.

"Johnson is my best friend. I'd never challenge him for the position, especially since I am a better fighter than he is. I'll support him and try to be as good of a beta as he was to me." Robby stood and started toward the door.

"If you ever need anything, please let us know."

He paused at the door. "The same holds true for you."

"Take care of that mate of yours."

He smiled, and this time it finally reached his eyes. "Bye." He slipped out the door, leaving me with the memories of his father.

CHAPTER 22

OUR LIFE SETTLED INTO a quiet routine. Archer and Cheryl moved into their home with the two children, but we got to watch them a couple of times a week when their work schedules conflicted.

Logan was more of a challenge than Kyle. He got into everything, and I wasn't fast enough in my wheelchair to head him off. But that kid was smart, even at four years old. And he could negotiate with the best of them.

The weekends were filled with Alessandra teaching Kyle alpha etiquette and me playing with Logan.

Some Saturdays were also used for the family to stretch their legs and test their speed in the woods. I longed for the ability to join them, but I reveled in Alessandra's joy flowing through our mate bond.

The pine scent filled my nostrils as I read the latest top thriller on my reader. The children's attempt at howling made me grin. They sounded so little and fierce. I sighed and re-read the same paragraph, wishing I was running with them.

A crack echoed, and my gaze jumped from the page to the woods. My heart thundered. There was no hunting on our property. Signs and fences prohibited it. But that definitely was a gunshot, wasn't it?

I glanced at the sky to make sure there weren't any thunder clouds around, but only the clear blue sky met my gaze. And there weren't any main roads near us for the sound of a car backfiring to be that clear.

Shock blanketed me through the bond, chilling me to the core. But at least it wasn't pain. Not at first. But when it came, a human cry followed from the woods. I didn't know who yelled out, but my heart rate went through the roof.

The need to go find out what was happening overrode logic. I shifted, falling out of the chair with a yelp as I dragged myself across the lawn using my front paws. My hind legs dragged behind me, as useless as my human legs. I let out a howl. A call for help.

It didn't take long for half a dozen wolves to tear through our yard toward the woods. One skidded to a stop and stared at me as I struggled to drag myself forward. He shifted and started toward me. It was one of Archer's friends.

"Mr. Blaez?"

I looked up at him and whined. I wanted to get to my wife and my son and my grandchildren, but my damned body wouldn't work. I forced the shift and lay sprawled on the ground, my breath heaving.

"Go." I pointed at the woods.

"At least let me help you get back to your chair." He pointed the few dozen yards back to the porch.

I considered ordering him to leave, but I'm sure if Alessandra came back and found me in this position, she'd have another concern to deal with. I knew she didn't need more chaos, so I nodded.

He stepped closer and paused.

"Just bring me the chair." I couldn't bring myself to let him pick me up.

He grabbed it and then placed it next to me. "Can I help?"

"I got it." I reached up and locked the wheel closest to me, and then rolled onto my back and pulled myself into a sitting position, using the chair as leverage. The act of getting into the chair occupied my mind, although it did nothing to calm my heart.

Sounds in the woods reached my ears as I situated my legs into place on the pads and then leaned back, huffing with the exertion. I unlocked the wheel and slowly rolled backward with my eyes locked on the tree line.

Alessandra ran out of the woods with Logan tucked in her arms and Kyle running after her in wolf form. Her eyes were wild, and they locked on me at the edge of the porch. Without a word, she dumped my grandson's body into my lap and turned to Kyle. "Stay here." Her command hit with all her alpha power, and she shifted, bounding back into the woods.

My fingers slipped under Logan's chin, searching for a pulse. It was strong and steady, despite the blood splattered all over him. His chest rose and fell in even beats, and just looking at the front of him didn't answer the millions of questions swarming my brain.

Kyle stared at the woods with a vacant gaze.

"What happened?" I asked.

Kyle didn't respond.

I felt along Logan's body, looking for the reason he was out cold, and I found it on the back of his head. A bump the size of an egg. I removed my fingers to be sure he wasn't bleeding.

"Kyle, what happened to your brother?" I asked more forcefully.

He finally looked at me and then down at the limp body in my arms. "Mom pushed him out of the way, and he hit a tree."

"Out of the way of what?" I squeezed the words out.

"A bullet."

I turned Logan to be sure there was no entry wound. The fact he had shifted back to human form wasn't lost on me. That sometimes happened with little ones when they were surprised or injured.

My brain caught up to his words. "Logan hit his head?"

Kyle shrugged and focused back on the woods. "Dad attacked the man with the gun."

The absence of emotion in his voice announced more than his words. I took in his pale cheeks and his near panting breath. I shifted Logan to my far shoulder and pulled Kyle into my lap, hugging him.

His young form shook as his calm demeanor shattered. He buried his face into my shoulder, and I held him as tight as I held Logan. The boy was in shock and needed a connection to hold onto.

"Shhh," I cooed in his ear as his sobs ramped up. I wasn't going to tell him it would be all right. Not with the dread stressing every muscle of mine.

Archer barreled out of the woods, holding Cheryl's limp wolf form in his arms. Tears streaked through the blood covering his cheeks and his steps became unsteady as his gaze found mine. Even from this distance, I could see the damage. Half of her head was missing.

No wonder Kyle had been numb. Not only had he seen his mother murdered, he also saw his father take out the killer.

"Where's your mother?" I asked Archer.

"She's getting rid of the bodies with the others." He fell to his knees on the grass. His voice hitched. "Fucking hunters were inside our fence."

A low growl came from deep in my throat. Pack lands had posted No Hunting signs all around the perimeter. It had been years since the last hunting incident, but that had been near the perimeter, and the hunters were not on our lands when they took the shot. And the result had not been a dead wolf.

He cradled his wife's body and rocked as his sorrow overcame him.

I held Kyle's head to my shoulder so he couldn't see and shielded Logan's eyes in case he woke up. I wished I could turn around and walk into the house with them, but the lip between the deck and the lawn was too great for me to roll backward.

An echo sounded over the woods, and Archer stiffened. His eyes widened, and he lay his wife on the ground and shot into the woods, shifting as he went.

Kyle growled in my arms. I could feel the struggle within him to break the command Alessandra gave.

No negative emotions leaked through the bond I had with Alessandra. No pain, nothing but mental anguish and a grim determination to finish the task at hand.

"Your grandmother is fine," I whispered to Kyle.

"How do you know?" He pulled away from my shoulder and met my gaze.

"I'm her mate, remember?" I lifted an eyebrow. "I don't feel the pure panic like before, just the resolve to get the job done and get home."

He settled in my lap and started to turn toward where his mother's body lay.

I turned his chin back toward me. "Nope. We are not going to look that way. But I need you to push the chair over the edge of the deck so we can get your brother inside and attended to, okay?"

Kyle nodded and slid his legs off my lap to the ground. With one push, I was on the wood and rolling backward easily. He jumped back into my lap, and I continued until I rolled over the threshold and into the house.

I headed to the couch, and Kyle helped me move Logan onto the cushions. I had him fetch me some water and some rags, and we cleaned the blood off his brother.

"Is he going to be okay?" Kyle asked when we were done.

"He hit his head pretty hard." I felt the knot again and sighed. "He's going to be dizzy for a couple of days, but he should be fine once his concussion goes away." I hoped I was right. I pulled my phone out of the side pocket of my chair and called the pack doctor, just in case. He'd need to come anyway to record Cheryl's death, so he could look at Logan to be sure there wasn't anything else ailing the child.

The doctor arrived at the house at the same time Alessandra and the rest of the pack came out of the woods. I watched from the window as he inspected Cheryl's body. When he started toward the house, Archer told him not to bother.

"Excuse me," I said from the doorway. "Logan needs to be looked at."

"It's his fault that she's dead," Archer growled, waving at Cheryl's body.

"She protected her young." Alessandra nodded for the doctor to proceed into the house.

"And she's dead because of that."

I rolled back, giving the doctor room to enter the house. I couldn't stomach Archer's reaction. I would gladly lay down my life for my grandchildren. And until this moment, I would have for Archer, but something fundamentally decent in him had broken.

"It wasn't Logan's fault," Kyle said as he looked at his little brother.

"No. It wasn't. Your father is just reacting to the situation."

When the doctor touched the knot on the back of Logan's head, the boy groaned and knocked his hand away. "That hurts."

"I bet," the doctor said. "Can you tell me your name?"

"Logan," he muttered and squinted his eyes open.

"That's right. Your grandpa will get you some ice for that bump and it should help." He stood and crossed to where I was, with Kyle by my side. "How long was he out?"

I glanced at the clock and made an educated guess based on when that first shot rang out. "No more than a half hour."

"Let him rest, but wake him up every couple of hours tonight to make sure he remembers his name. He might need darkening shades in his room. And limit his time on the electronics for a few days. He should be back to normal in a couple of weeks."

"Thanks, Doc." I shook his hand.

Kyle followed him out the back door, and I rolled into the kitchen and got one of our flexible ice packs. When I set it gently on Logan's head, he hissed at me.

"This will help." I kept my hand in place.

"I think something happened to my mom," he said in a whisper. "I don't feel her connection anymore." His pain-filled eyes met mine.

I nodded. "She saved you." I bopped his nose gently. "And I'm sure she is happy that you are okay."

His eyes misted over. "But my dad isn't happy."

"He is happy that you are okay, but he is sad and angry that your mom died. It's going to be tough going for a while." I stroked his forehead.

A tear slipped from his eye, and sadness blanketed over me. The slider closed, and I glanced over my shoulder.

Alessandra stepped inside with a blanket over her shoulders. Her puffy eyes carried the red from crying, and she sniffled.

"Go wash up. I've got this one."

"Colin said you shifted." She wiped her nose on the edge of the blanket.

I nodded. "I didn't get very far."

"He said you were almost to the wood line." She stepped away and came back with sweatpants for me.

I turned the chair away from Logan and shimmied into the pants as best I could. "Thanks. Now you need to clean up while I get some dinner going for us." I pointed toward the bedroom. "And let Archer know we'll keep watch over Logan tonight."

She didn't argue with me. She slipped into the bedroom and the shower went on.

"What would you like for dinner?" I asked Logan.

His four-year-old frown looked more like an old man's. "Nothing."

"Maybe a ginger ale and some crackers?"

He made a noncommittal noise and closed his eyes.

I retrieved some saltines and a small can of soda along with a straw, so Logan wouldn't have to move. My stomach never did well with concussions either, but a little soda and a few crackers always seemed to settle it down enough to be comfortable.

ALESSANDRA TUCKED LOGAN INTO Archer's old bed while I cleaned up and slid into our bed.

We hadn't talked about what happened yet. Not with our grandson in the room. I set the alarm clock for a couple of hours to wake him like the doctor suggested and waited for my wife.

She cracked the bedroom door and slid under the sheets before moving next to me. She nuzzled into the crook of my arm. "Archer wants nothing to do with Logan."

"Doesn't he get that if she hadn't pushed him out of the way, they'd be mourning a child?"

"No. He's so wrapped up in hurt, he's lashing out at his son. He needs to blame someone, and it's easier to focus his anger on the one his wife saved than on the trespassing hunters he killed." She sighed. "Well, he killed one and left the other to die from his wounds. We put that bastard down before we dumped the bodies in the ravine."

"There will be blowback." The human world always cried foul when a human was killed, even if it was because of their own stupidity. "I'll call the council members in the morning and inform them of the situation."

"Make sure the council knows they were trespassing. And they weren't from around here. According to their licenses, they were from Kentucky. Plus, their cooler was full of empty beers, so I gather they were drunk to boot."

"Idiots," I muttered.

"It's all in the ravine, so it might take awhile to be reported."

KYLE JOINED LOGAN AT our house the next day because Archer was inconsolable and unavailable emotionally to address his children's needs.

After a week, Logan was well enough to go back to nursery school, and I rolled down to Archer's house without Alessandra. It was time for a little tough love because he could not wallow in mourning with children.

I banged on the door and waited. As each minute passed, my frustration mounted. If I wasn't stuck in this wheelchair, I would have kicked in the door by now. "Archer?" I called and banged my fist on the door again.

Finally, the door opened, and Archer squinted out at me.

He looked like he hadn't slept or ate since Cheryl died. I got a whiff of him and added bathing to the list of things he had avoided.

"What the fuck, Archer?" I waved at him.

"My wife died," he snarled.

"I know. But you didn't die, and your children need you."

He waved his hand at me. "Like you wouldn't just crawl in a hole and die if Mom was killed."

"I would die for her or you or those kids in a second. And I know your mom would do the same for me." She risked her life to save me, but I didn't need to tell him that at this moment. "If she died, I would feel like crawling in a hole, but I wouldn't because it would spit in the face of all she is to me."

He recoiled.

"I would mourn her, no doubt about that, but I would keep moving, keep breathing, keep living in her honor. With kids, you do not have the luxury of shutting the world out, or slowly killing yourself." I waved at him. "Cheryl would be pissed at you for neglecting your kids all week, especially since she died protecting one of them." I let that settle.

Archer ran his hand through his hair and the greasy ends stuck out as if they were sprayed stiff. "I can't."

"I'm giving you another day to sleep and get your shit together before I send your mother down here to order you to function for your kids." I took a breath to calm my rising anger. "If I don't see you up at the house tomorrow, you'll get that visit." I rolled away with my heart

pounding and my teeth grinding until my jaw
ached.

CHAPTER 23

THE NEXT DAY BEFORE school let out, the front door squeaked open. I looked up from the book I was reading and exhaled, letting all the tension that had built through the day go.

Archer stepped into the room, bathed and in decent clothing. He sheepishly shoved his hands into his pockets. "You were right."

"Every once in a while, that happens."

Alessandra snorted from the seat next to me.

"But I have to be honest. I'm not sure how I'm going to react to Logan."

"You are blaming him for what an illegal trespasser did? That is not okay," Alessandra snapped.

"If he had just stayed put—" Archer started.

Alessandra was on her feet and in his face in a blink. "We all wanted to run. It wasn't just Logan, so don't you dare blame that boy." She poked him in the chest. "We run all the time."

"But—"

"No buts allowed on this. If you want to put blame anywhere, it's on those dead assholes who trespassed on our lands and ignored all the posted signs just to get a wolf pelt. And you already had your vengeance on them."

"And the council absolved you of any wrongdoing where those trespassers were concerned," I added, just so he knew he was in the right in the council's eyes. If they had passed any other judgment on my son, I would have pulled favors to hide him while I got him a new identification so he wouldn't have to face a death sentence.

Alessandra shot me a glare. She had been grilled by the council members about what had happened before they rendered judgment.

"If he hadn't begged—"

"He's four."

"He's going to challenge Kyle someday, and I'm going to lose him, too!" Archer blew up.

"It doesn't work that way in our pack." Alessandra crossed her arms. "Logan may be a powerful alpha in his own right, but he can never lead this pack. Not without the mark. So all these fears you're brewing are not valid."

Archer sat down and covered his face, but he stopped spouting off excuses, even though his frustration boiled under the surface. The front door opened, and he recovered quickly. He wiped his face and leaned back in the chair.

Kyle stepped into the room with Logan at his side. He had been tasked with coming home with his brother instead of at his normal time to help us out.

"Daddy," Logan cried and ran toward him, but skidded to a stop before he crashed into his father. That joyous burst fizzled.

I wanted to smack my son for the chill in the air.

"How was school?" Archer looked from Logan to Kyle, clearly dismissing the younger child.

"Good," Kyle said. "Why don't you tell Dad about your project?" he said to Logan, trying to keep his younger brother in the conversation.

Kyle was being the perfect pack leader by including Logan in the conversation. It saddened me that his father couldn't offer that same type of support.

Logan launched into his day like any enthusiastic four-year-old, entertaining all of us with his antics...except his father, who stared on with a stoic expression, only brightening up when Kyle spoke.

CHAPTER 24

ARCHER NEVER DID WARM up to Logan again. His parenting style varied from offering sharp feedback to ignoring Logan altogether while he praised Kyle whenever possible. It seemed Cheryl's death always loomed between them, no matter how many years passed. And Archer never fully recovered from her loss.

When Kyle was twenty, Alessandra passed the alpha position to him, and I recommended Archer as my replacement on the council, hoping that would thaw the bitterness that had crept in and made a home in his heart.

The council requested a transition period that would include both me and Alessandra in attendance for at least the first meeting and then in an advisory capacity at meetings until we were fully ready to step away and retire.

I scoffed at the idea, but Alessandra thought there was some merit in her advising Kyle until he was a little older and more experienced.

As the annual council meeting started, I scanned the alphas. Most remained the same as they'd always been. But there were a handful of transitions happening, especially considering we were all getting on in age. Frankly, we wanted to relax and let someone else lead for a change.

Just before Archer pounded the gavel to start the meeting, the door opened and Robby Young slipped inside without his alpha. His commanding presence blanketed all of us, and he offered a smile of embarrassment for cutting it close. Another minute and he would have been considered late.

His gaze found mine, and I gave him a nod from my position between Archer and Alessandra at the table. He acknowledged it with a tilt of his chin.

The council went through normal business updates, including Archer's appointment to the council and Kyle's promotion to alpha within the pack, and then Archer asked whether there were any other items to discuss.

Robby stepped forward and cleared his throat before speaking. "As you all know, Rick Johnson passed away a few weeks ago." Murmurs and nods filled the room. "I'd like to take the position of alpha for the Allegany pack again."

Archer's face scrunched with distaste. "Your mate wasn't a wolf."

My gaze snapped to my son. I don't know where the hell that prejudice came from, but it irked me. He had mentioned it once when Robby and Rick had informed the council of the demise of the Monster Defense Agency. Both Alessandra and I had been disappointed then, and from the look on her face right now, we were in that headspace again.

I never cared who someone mated with. I only cared that they were decent and respectful and put their pack first.

"What the hell does that have to do with me taking over as alpha?"

Robby's question was valid, and we all turned our attention to Archer.

"You have half-breed children."

Robby's face turned red, and the growl that came out of him made me quiver. "Again, what does that have to do with leading my pack?"

I had enough of this prejudice bullshit.

"Robby is an exceptional alpha." I shot a glare at my son and his unacceptable behavior before I addressed the rest of the alphas in the room. "He led the pack for years before his captivity. And they thrived under his exceptional leadership. When he was thought to be dead, his best friend and beta was named alpha. Upon Robby's return, he did not challenge his friend. Instead, he honored Rick's station as alpha and operated as the pack beta all these years." I paused and scanned the room. I didn't know one alpha in this room who wouldn't do the same for their beta if they were in the same circumstance. "I do not have a problem with Robby Young taking over the pack again."

Out of the corner of my eye, I saw the other council members nodding.

My son's glare made me wonder whether I had made the right decision about offering him the council position. If he couldn't be just and compassionate, then the council wouldn't be as effective as we were for all these years.

"All in favor," Archer said through clenched teeth. Everyone but Archer raised their hand.

He didn't bother asking for any opposed show of hands. He would have been the only one in the room who didn't approve of the ask.

"Motion approved," he grumbled. "Anything else?" When no one stepped forward, he said, "Meeting adjourned."

I rolled out from behind the table with my anger simmering. I approached Robby before he left the room. "I'm sorry about that." I hooked my thumb back toward the table where the council was still talking.

"I'm used to it. How are you doing?"

"Tired lately." I smiled and shrugged. My ailments drained me on a daily basis, but I wasn't going to give Robby a rundown of my failing health. "How are your kids?" I thought back to the one time I met them. Unfortunately, it was at their mother's funeral, but his daughter was the cutest thing I had ever seen. I even treated her to a wheelie in my chair before Alessandra scolded me into behaving for the rest of the funeral.

"They are good. It was a tough go for a while, but I think they've been able to move forward without their mother." He ran his hand through his hair. "I appreciate that you and your wife came to Sarah's funeral. I'm not sure I said that to you."

"No need to thank us. We are always here for our friends." I looked him over. Outside the dark circles under his eyes, he appeared to be solidly in control of his emotions. "You seem to be doing okay, too."

He shrugged. "I don't have the luxury of wallowing in sorrow. I have two kids who need me and a pack that needs a leader."

And that was why I backed him for the position.

He lost his wife a while ago and then his best friend a few weeks ago, and he wasn't thinking of his loss. No, his focus was on his children and his pack.

CHAPTER 25

"HEY GRANDPA," LOGAN SAID as he waltzed into the room with his legal attaché case under his arm.

I pressed the button on the bed, lifting the head of my side of the mattress up to take him in. My health had taken a sharp turn recently, and the doctor wasn't optimistic. It seemed the paralysis finally caught up to me, with infections and kidney failure. "You delivering subpoenas again?"

"Yup." He smiled. "I need money for a car and my dad thought this would help with my college resume."

"He's right." At least Archer had pressed Logan to go to school and make something of himself instead of continuing to beat the boy down on a daily basis.

Logan sat next to me and leaned his elbows on his knees. "I need to ask you a question."

"Okay." I smiled, even though I felt like death warmed over. "What can I help you with?"

He shifted in the seat and cocked his head as if trying to figure out how to ask. "Do you think I'll ever be alpha?"

"You would make a superb alpha, but that isn't in the cards in this pack." He knew his brother held the mark of a leader and that he could never challenge him and be accepted as the alpha of our pack.

He deflated before me as if I just shot his dreams to hell. He stared at his folded hands.

I couldn't let him give up his dreams. "Logan, the world is a big place."

His head snapped up, and he met my gaze.

I smiled and continued. "You should find your place to shine. You are strong. Stronger than your brother. But the gods chose him to mark as alpha of this pack."

"Are you telling me to leave?" Hurt filled his voice.

"To reach your full potential, yes." I knew it was hard for him to hear. This was his home, and everything he loved was here within our pack.

He blinked a sudden mist out of his eyes and his chin trembled.

"Look, Logan. I love you with all my heart. I don't want to see you go, but I also don't want you to become a bitter shell like your father. You have a mate somewhere out there. Find her and find your place as an alpha. If an opportunity presents itself, don't pass it up to live in your brother's shadow, or worse, live as a rogue because you can't be a follower."

"Who says I can't be a follower?" He crossed his arms and leaned back in the chair with a stubborn jut of his chin.

I raised an eyebrow at him. Logan was a natural leader and could be even more cocky than his grandmother. He was not prone to submission, even when ordered to, and that had caused a lot of sibling scraps between him and Kyle over the years. Even when Alessandra was alpha, once he hit thirteen, he could ignore her orders, which reminded me too much of myself. I could ignore Alessandra for days on end if I didn't agree with her, but I still felt the sting of her orders whether I liked it or not. But I never saw a flinch in Logan when he ignored her or his brother's directives.

As his brother put it, Logan was almost too perfect not to be a leader somewhere. And I prayed he'd get that chance someday.

"Are you scared?" he asked, pulling me out of my reverie.

The worry and sadness in his eyes tightened my throat, and I thought about the question.

Was I scared to die?

My wheelchair caught my eye. Fifty years tied to that miserable thing was long enough. I slowly shook my head.

"I've been able to help a lot of people over the years. And I've had a full life with the woman I love more than life itself." I smiled. "And as a beautiful bonus, I've seen my grandchildren grow into fine young men."

"That's because of you."

I didn't argue. Their father had become a ball of bitterness that none of us really could stomach being around for long. I didn't know whether the man had smiled or laughed since his wife died, and I didn't know why he couldn't get out of his own way to see that there were people around him who cared.

I shrugged. "I've had a good run, Logan. Just remember what the important things in life are as you navigate this world."

"I will. I love you, Grandpa."

He leaned over and kissed my cheek. The sheen in his eyes nearly overflowed. He squeezed my hand and hurried out of the room, grabbing his bag before he left without another look back. But his sorrow lingered on the air.

ALESSANDRA CAME INTO THE room after Logan left. She carried a plate of food, and I shook my head. That shit wouldn't stay down, and I didn't want to throw up again.

I had said my peace to Archer and Kyle earlier in the day before they went off to work. But I hung on to speak with Logan. I am glad he asked me the question first, because telling him he should look for opportunities outside the pack with no lead-in would have been more like a sledgehammer than a suggestion.

My time was coming. My body ached with fever, and my organs were slowly shutting down on me. I would have rather gone in my sleep, but I didn't have that luxury.

Dying wasn't fun in any condition. But it was time.

I reached out, took Alessandra's hand in mine and brought it to my lips, kissing it tenderly before I pulled her toward me and captured her mouth in a lingering kiss. I wanted to taste her forever.

She pulled back, and concern crinkled her forehead. "I love you, Jacob Blaez."

Darkness edged my vision, but the tear slipping from the corner of her eye captivated me. "Don't cry, baby. Just think about the next time I see you. I will dance with you and run with you and make sweet, sweet love to you. I promise we will take advantage of all that heaven offers." I smiled. "I love you, Leigh."

My vision faded into overwhelming brightness, and with my last breath, I muttered, "I'll see you on the other side."

THE END

About J.E. Taylor

J.E. Taylor is a USA Today bestselling author, a publisher, an editor, a manuscript formatter, a mother, a wife, a retired business analyst, and a Supernatural fangirl. Not necessarily in that order. She first sat down to seriously write in February of 2007 after her daughter asked:

"Mom, if you could do anything, what would you do?"

From that moment on, she hasn't looked back.

Besides being co-owner of Novel Concept Publishing, Ms. Taylor also moonlights as a Senior Editor of Allegory E-zine, an online venue for Science Fiction, Fantasy and Horror.

She lives in New Hampshire with her husband and during the summer months enjoys her weekends on the shore in southern Maine.

Visit her at www.jetaylor75.com and sign up for her newsletter for early previews of her upcoming books, release announcements, and special opportunities for free swag!

You can also buy J.E. Taylor's books direct
on her website here:
https://books.jetaylor75.com/